'Stop!' Lizz...
muffled by t...

'What's the matte... ...uch as I do...' Nick said, ...voice bruised with desire.

'No...' she said shakily. 'You're wrong.'

He made a low noise of dissent. 'I'm not. You've just told me as much with your mouth, your body—and, one way or another, you've been telling me since you arrived.'

Dear Reader

For many of us, this is the best period of the year—the season of goodwill and celebration—though it can make big demands on your time and pocket, too! Or, maybe you prefer to spend these mid-winter months more quietly? Whatever you've got planned, Mills & Boon's romances are always there for you as special friends at the turn of the year: easy, entertaining and comforting reads that are great value for money. Stay warm, won't you!

The Editor

Jenny Cartwright was born and raised in Wales. After three years at University in Kent and a year spent in America, she returned to Wales where she has lived and worked ever since. Happily married with three young children—a girl and two boys—she began to indulge her lifelong desire to write when her lively twins were very small. The peaceful solitude she enjoys while creating her romances contrasts happily with the often hectic bustle of her family life.

RELUCTANT SURRENDER

BY

JENNY CARTWRIGHT

MILLS & BOON LIMITED
ETON HOUSE   18-24 PARADISE ROAD
RICHMOND   SURREY   TW9 1SR

First published in Great Britain 1992
by Mills & Boon Limited

© Jenny Cartwright 1992

Australian copyright 1992
Philippine copyright 1992
This edition 1993

ISBN 0 263 77866 5

Set in Times Roman 10 on 12 pt.
01-9301-53234 C

Made and printed in Great Britain

CHAPTER ONE

THE wretched van had stalled. Lizzy slammed one foot hard on the brake, while she yanked on the handbrake with all her strength. She just didn't trust this miserable vehicle. It had been grumbling ever since she'd left the main road and had taken to the rutted mountain track. She kept her foot pressed firmly to the floor, convinced that if she once eased the pressure the wheels would start to roll and the van, complete with all her worldly possessions, not to mention herself, would career backwards over the edge of the hairpin bend. And then everybody back home would have the undoubted pleasure of saying 'I told you so'. Which in a funny sort of way presented a far more dispiriting prospect than that of her own untimely demise.

She tried the ignition. The van wheezed and juddered slightly, but clearly had no intention of restarting. The more she tried, the more determinedly it coughed itself back into inertia. 'Come on, you stupid beast!' she hissed between clenched teeth. 'Start, damn you!'

She glared at the almost human face of its instrument panel. The speedometer stared sullenly back at her, like the solitary eye of a sour old man. It was clearly as sick and tired of this journey as she was. Two days of non-stop driving, not to mention a night cuddled up in the back of the van with two hundredweight of clay, had temporarily managed to flatten even Lizzy's buoyant spirits. The van, which had seemed all right when she had purchased it just a few days ago, was now obviously at the end of its tether.

Even with the side-windows open the inside of the van was scorchingly hot. Her sunglasses, slippery with sweat, slid down her short, freckled nose for the umpteenth time. She raised one hand from the steering-wheel, wiped the palm down the length of one slender, denim-clad thigh, and then pushed the spectacles back with a weary gesture. She stuck her head out of the open window. A hint of a breeze ruffled her bedraggled pony-tail, but left her face as burningly hot as ever.

Over her shoulder she could see the blue, misty landscape of the mountains of southern France unfolding into the distance. The switchback road had carried her high into the world of tiny villages and ragged sheep and mad-eyed goats. She groaned. It was all very well admiring the view, but it was quite another matter being stuck in the middle of it in a thoroughly untrustworthy van, with your foot aching from pressing down on the brake, your T-shirt sticking to your skin, and your AA membership invalid on this side of *La Manche*. And the worst of it was, there was nothing she could do to help herself. Or at least, not without taking her foot off the brake, which she was convinced would precipitate her into oblivion. The trouble was, she reflected uncomfortably, she was so used to being self-reliant that when moments like this arrived she felt utterly lost. She tried the key in the ignition again. Nothing. She must be practically there by now. You'd think the van might have waited!

Her sunglasses were beginning yet another descent of her nose. Infuriated, she thrust them high up on to her unruly mass of red curls, rubbing the sweat away from her eyes as she did so. Any minute now she would collapse from heat exhaustion. Her foot would clunk on to the floor and...

'*Bonjour, mademoiselle. Est-ce que je peux vous aider?*'

She had no idea where he had sprung from. He certainly hadn't been there a moment ago. She glanced at his feet. He was wearing a pair of rope-soled espadrilles, ideal for padding about in silently, and very French. Oh, well, who cared from whence he came? He was here, like a knight on a white charger, and that was all that mattered.

'*Er... Oui, merci, monsieur. S'il vous plaît...*' She struggled with her rusty French as she sized up the man who had appeared so fortuitously from nowhere. He was distinctly Gallic, with the long, blunt nose and cynical smile that she associated with men of his race. His skin was olive, burnt dark by the sun. She turned her eyes away from his crisp, dark curls and forced herself to concentrate instead on his biceps. Yes, he was certainly muscular enough to push the van further up the road, and, being somewhere in his mid-thirties, not so old that she need fear the exertion would finish him off. Perfect.

'*L'auto...*' she began. '*Er... l'auto ne marche pas. Il est*—er—defunct.'

He laughed, revealing an astonishingly perfect set of even white teeth. His grey eyes crinkled attractively at the corners. Hmmm. She was beginning to feel better already.

'Petrol,' he said. 'I can smell petrol.'

'*Ah. L'essence. Oui. Vous pouvez...*' Now what *was* the French verb for smell? '*Vous pouvez sentir l'essence...*'

'Why are you translating my words into French?'

She looked at him, blinking foolishly. 'Er—so you can understand them . . .' she explained earnestly, tailing off as she belatedly grasped his point. She must be more tired than she had thought! Their eyes met. Simultaneously they started to laugh.

Lizzy stopped laughing first. The pain in her foot was becoming serious. 'Look,' she began, 'I don't think the handbrake is up to much on this old heap. I've been sitting here for hours with my foot pressed to the floor. I think I'm going to get cramp in a moment.'

'Seven minutes,' he responded drily.

'*Sept minutes*. That one's easy to translate, but I haven't a clue what it means.'

'It means you've been sitting here for seven minutes. That's all. I saw you from my garden. I've been timing you.'

'Oh . . .' So he lived near here. He must practically be a neighbour. His English was awfully good. It would come in useful, having someone on the spot who could help her translate.

'I can still smell petrol. I think you must have flooded the engine trying to restart it. Quite a feat in this heat.'

'Oh . . .' His English really was superb. Scarcely a trace of an accent. 'So what does that mean?'

'It means you can try pushing the accelerator to the floor . . .' He went on to give her explicit instructions for restarting the engine. Instructions which, moreover, worked!

She started to move at a snail's pace, just to test it out, and then stopped again to stick her head out of the window to thank him.

'Any time,' he murmured, his eyes glinting ambiguously, then added, 'That hill start was fine. The handbrake must be OK. What made you think it wasn't?'

She nodded at the speedometer, and was about to explain about the spiteful looks it had been giving her when she suddenly thought better of it. 'I—er—I just didn't trust it...' she muttered. Well, he might think her mechanical knowledge was a bit deficient—which was, after all, no more than the truth—but at least he wouldn't think she was crazy. Though why she should care what he thought of her she couldn't imagine.

'Why didn't you put it into gear?' he asked drily. 'The wheels couldn't have rolled backwards then.'

She groaned, then cast him an apologetic smile. Inwardly she was cringing. If only she'd remembered that little fact she could have set off on foot to look for aid, instead of sitting there waiting to be rescued. It was all very well depending on French knights on *chevaux blancs* when there was no choice. But she didn't want him to think she was entirely helpless.

'Do you know a house round here called Mon Abri?' she asked hurriedly, to hide her confusion.

'Mon Abri? Of course. It's up ahead, beyond the bend—less than a couple of hundred yards...' He paused briefly, then added mockingly, '*Moins de deux cent mètres ...*'

'Oh, great!' she cried, her spirits soaring at last. She really was almost there! She revved the engine loudly to avoid the possibility of stalling again. He was saying something else to her, but she couldn't make it out. She just nodded vaguely and waved him a cheerful farewell.

He shrugged, then, giving her a brief salute, walked briskly away. She watched his back view disappearing.

The well-fitting, well-worn jeans, white polo shirt—good quality and pristine-clean—navy espadrilles and that delectable coating of sleek, fine dark hairs along the line of his muscular forearms moved rapidly into the middle distance. He was astonishingly attractive, in a distinctly European kind of way.

She wrinkled her nose in dismay as she found her thoughts wandering up the road with him. She was here to set up in business. That was *all*. She'd promised herself that nothing was going to distract her. Nor would it.

Not that she was about to be distracted by a man, whatever the circumstances. Lizzy had abandoned her half-hearted attempts at romance some three years earlier, when the man with whom she'd been trying hard to fall in love had unceremoniously dumped her, claiming that she was enough to drive any man insane. Which was pretty much what her first boyfriend had said on a similar occasion.

Anna, her best friend and flatmate through the student years, had told her she should put it down to bad luck, and not let the experience embitter her.

'You don't understand, Anna,' she had explained stoically. 'I'm not a bit heartbroken. And not the least bitter. Just realistic. I'm afraid I'm too—well, I don't know... a bit too gritty... too intense, certainly, to make someone the perfect wife.'

'Rubbish. You're far and away the nicest person I know,' Anna had responded warmly, adding, 'I'll bet there's some dishy little wimp waiting just around the next corner, who can't wait to be bossed around by you for the rest of his life!'

Lizzy had laughed good-humouredly, but there was too much truth in the remark for comfort. The trouble was, she didn't want to spend her days issuing orders to a wimp—no matter how dishy he might be. No. She'd made up her mind to do without men, and so far she was convinced she'd made the right decision. She loved her life—her work—and quite frankly she didn't want anything more.

She crashed the engine into gear and set off to find Mon Abri. The gates were just as she'd remembered— a fresh, glossy white. The house too, or what she could see of it through the gates, looked newly painted and in good condition. Dear old Jean-Claude and Marie had obviously taken Grandma's injunction to 'keep an eye on the place' very much to heart. Admittedly Grandma had sent them a small monthly sum to cover expenses, but it wouldn't have come anywhere near the true cost of keeping the old place this smart. She must find a way to reward them once she started earning some money.

She felt her heart swell with pride. *Her* house. It was hard to believe that it was her house now. A roaring pleasure thundered through her. She had arrived home, at last.

It took her a few minutes to open the gates, drive up to the forecourt in front of the house, and close the gates again. Walking back to the van, she noticed that the driveway had been recently gravelled. The garden was blooming lavishly, and the old stone house beneath its mellow pan-tiled roof had spanking new green shutters at every window. Lizzy frowned. Since she had inherited the house she had taken it upon herself to make the monthly maintenance payment to the local couple who had cooked and cleaned for Grandma and herself when they had holidayed there. There was no way that the frugal amount could have paid for all this! She'd been expecting to find the place half-derelict. What on earth was going on?

A worrying doubt began to uncurl in her mind. She hastily fumbled in her bag for the big key to the front door. It turned smoothly. Cautiously pushing open the door, she peered nervously inside. Honestly, anyone would think she was an intruder instead of the owner! Summoning her courage, she stepped smartly inside and looked around. The proportions of the lovely, airy room hadn't changed a bit. But the stripped and varnished floors, the gaily coloured ethnic rugs, the huge cream-coloured sofas all were new. A half-read novel lay open but face-down on one of the sofas.

'Someone,' she said boldly, in attempt to chivvy her flagging confidence into life, 'has been eating my porridge.'

'I thought Goldilocks was a blonde?' came a resonantly deep voice from the doorway.

Her heart began to drum ominously. She turned around. It was him. And he was leaning against the door-jamb as if he owned the place. The bright sunlight behind him cast his face into shadow, so that she couldn't make out his expression.

'Oh . . .' she said, her mouth dry. 'I—er—the thing is, this is *my* house. But it looks as if someone else is living here.'

'Yes,' he agreed, his voice an amused growl.

She swallowed hard. 'I take it that you're the someone?'

'Yes . . .' he agreed again. And again there was something wry in the tone of his voice. He obviously felt very much at home, and quite unperturbed by her announcement.

It annoyed her. However he had come to be here—
and, from the little she had seen of the house's stun-
ningly transformed interior, he had been here for quite
a while—he must know that he had no right to be in this
place. No right at all, she sternly reminded herself.

She straightened her back and took a few steps towards him. 'Let me introduce myself. My name is Lizzy
Braithewaite.'

She couldn't help the self-mocking note that crept into
her voice whenever she spoke her name aloud. There
was something so absurdly pretentious about the sound
of it. This time, however, she could have kicked herself
for the denigrating intonation that had automatically
coloured the words.

'I think,' she continued, her voice firmer as she let
her eyes draw his lazy gaze, 'that I must be your new
landlady.'

His eyes didn't falter. They continued to meet hers
with a relaxed humour glinting in their grey depths. As
if the two of them were sharing some private joke. She
looked away.

'I'm very pleased to meet you, Miss *Braithewaite*,' he
responded at length, mimicking her mocking tone. He
stepped towards her and unexpectedly grasped her right
hand in both of his. Her creamy skin looked almost
translucent, sandwiched between his broad, sun-tanned
hands. Her eyes were drawn to those sleek, fine black
hairs, running down the line of the muscle from elbow
to wrist. She couldn't help observing approvingly that
his hands weren't hairy at all.

'Or may I call you Lizzy?'

Her hand was still locked between his. His touch was
light and dry, and she was suddenly uncomfortably aware

of how hot and moist her own must feel. She wanted to tug it away, but he was holding her surprisingly firmly. She didn't want to make her discomfiture too obvious.

'If you like,' she conceded with as light a touch as she could manage. 'And what shall I call you, Monsieur...?'

'Nick Holt,' he said laconically. 'I'm not French, you know. I'm as English as toast and marmalade.'

'But you've got French arms!' The words had escaped from her lips before she'd had a chance to think. She dragged her hand free and clamped it over her mouth. What an unbelievably stupid thing to have said!

He caught his lower lip lightly between his teeth, while the corners of his mouth curled with amusement. Then he tilted his head slightly, surveyed his arms and shrugged mildly. 'It must be all the garlic in the food...' he murmured.

She puffed out an irritated sigh. 'Look, could we just get back to the subject of the house?'

He locked his fingers behind his neck, letting his gaze run over her quizzically. 'All right,' he sighed as if it were a matter of no real consequence. 'Let me fetch a bottle of wine from the fridge, and then we can sit out in the garden and relax while you explain to me how you've come to be my...? Aaah, yes...my landlady.'

'Wine?' she said suspiciously.

'Yes, that's right. You're in France now, you know?'

'But it's four o'clock in the afternoon.'

'This isn't England. Puritanism never made much of an impact on this side of the Channel,' he said drily, adding cryptically as he headed into the kitchen, 'And *vive la difference*...'

She watched his back view disappearing, her eyes wary. Jean-Claude and Marie must be leasing him the house.

It was an awful cheek, but understandable in its way. No doubt they would have approached Grandma about it if she hadn't been such a daunting character. Anyway, if the rent had paid for all these improvements, she could hardly complain! Nick Holt probably thought his tenancy was all above board and quite secure...

Perhaps the relaxed atmosphere engendered by the wine would be a good idea. After all, he probably knew nothing about the ownership of Mon Abri. If she was going to have to evict him, she'd have to be very tactful. A quality for which she was not exactly noted, she acknowledged with a heartfelt sigh.

'I'm parched,' she called through to him. 'You couldn't bring me some water as well, could you?'

He led her out through the french doors on to the shady terrace beneath the veranda, where a simple pine table and rattan chairs were waiting for them. It wasn't until she was sitting comfortably in the cool shade that she realised how rigidly she had been holding herself. She relaxed into the contours of the chair. Suddenly she felt absolutely drained. It had been a very long couple of days. But the water was deliciously cold and refreshing. It made her feel almost human again. And the bunch of dusky dark green grapes, and the bread and cheese he had brought to accompany the wine made her mouth water.

'So you're my new landlady?' he asked evenly, surveying her across the top of his wine glass.

She nodded cautiously. 'It would seem so. My grandmother died seven weeks ago. This was her house, and she left it to me in her will.'

'Uh huh...' he responded, nodding thoughtfully. 'All the formalities—probate and so on—they can't have been completed so soon?'

She shook her head vigorously, so that her carelessly knotted pony-tail began to collapse sideways. She lifted one hand to free her tangled mass of red curls. 'No,' she agreed, shaking her hair down on to her shoulders. 'Look, I know I've been a bit—well, precipitate in coming out here so soon. But it's going to take an awfully long time for the will to be proved, and I was desperate to get out here and start working. But I'm sure we can sort something out between us.'

'And did the solicitors not advise you——?'

'Of course they did!' she interrupted, exasperated by his continuing coolness in the face of her arrival. She was finding all this horribly unsettling. Surely he should be just a little perturbed, too?

'Look, Mr—er—Nick.' If he was going to call her Lizzy, then she wanted to put things on an even footing. He already seemed to have gained the upper hand, simply by putting the food on the table. 'This is my house now. I had every right to come out here to work. If I'd realised you were here, of course it might have put a different complexion on things. But I had no idea.'

He nodded thoughtfully. 'So you *were* advised to wait?'

'Advised to wait? Practically everybody I'd ever met advised me to wait! They wanted me to sell this place when the time came. And until then just to plod along in my little rut till the day finally arrived when I could set up my business in a sensible way that wouldn't embarrass *them*.

'But,' she lifted her elfin chin high in the air, 'I wouldn't be told by them. So don't you try telling me, either, because you'll be wasting your breath. I'm congenitally incapable of taking advice.'

He laughed, showing his perfect teeth again. But this time it was a laugh which he deliberately cut short. 'Nevertheless, Lizzy, you have been a bit too hasty. No doubt if you'd waited you'd have discovered that things aren't as straightforward as you've believed.'

'If I'd waited for the solicitors to OK everything,' she exclaimed humorously, 'you'd be looking at someone with advanced middle-age spread! You see, my grandmother was a rather...unusual woman. She didn't believe in solicitors and banks and all that sort of thing. She drew up her will herself. The lawyers say that it looks as if she made quite a good job of it, but it will take a very long time for it to all be finally confirmed. I'm afraid I couldn't possibly have waited that long, and I couldn't see any harm in coming straight out here...'

He was looking steadily at her, his grey eyes unflinching. What was the matter with him? The more she told him, the less concerned he seemed. He was just sitting there, thinking, his features quite impassive.

'Don't worry,' she said seriously, realising with a spurt of relief why he was looking so grave. 'I won't evict you without giving you proper notice and everything! I'm sorry. I should have made things plainer from the start. But I'm sure we can come to some sort of sensible agreement. Jean-Claude and Marie were a bit...well... Let's just say that they probably didn't make things very clear when they let you rent the house.'

'Jean-Claude?' he queried, his eyes losing their even expression, and becoming surprisingly shrewd.

'Grandma's been sending him and his wife a small monthly sum to keep an eye on the house. I expect they——'

'Jean-Claude's been a widower for some years. I'm afraid he's not the man he was without his wife to keep him up to scratch.' He sounded distinctly disapproving.

'Lizzy,' he continued, meeting her eyes purposefully, 'it looks as if things are a little more complicated than you imagine. I'm afraid you aren't going to be able to live here.'

She waited for him to continue. It was only natural that he'd want to defend his right to go on inhabiting the place. But she wasn't going to allow herself to get het up about it. She had arrived, after all. That was the important thing. She could easily set up her pottery in the out-buildings at the back, just as she'd planned, and even live out there for a couple of months during the summer while he was in residence. She could make it quite comfy... Just as long as she could get her business going she didn't much care about the practicalities. And anyway, the house was in such superb condition... That was a wonderful bonus. She'd expected to be more or less camping out in it as it was, so she could hardly complain if she didn't have free access to all the luxury she'd glimpsed within. She lifted a cluster of grapes to her mouth.

He straightened in his chair. 'Those grapes are the exact same colour as your eyes!' he commented. 'Though your eyes have got a beautiful charcoal line around the iris...'

She was taken aback, until she realised that he was simply trying to change the subject. Which, of course, was understandable. She'd no idea how long he'd been leasing the place, but it must be quite a while. Hadn't he mentioned something about 'his garden' in a proprietorial kind of way? He certainly seemed very much at home. So, however calm he seemed, he must be having some kind of an inner struggle, assimilating this new turn of events. She bit the inside of her full, lower lip, wondering how to get him to understand.

'You don't need to flatter me,' she said ruefully at last. 'I'm really not going to chuck you out, as I said, or at least——'

'Lizzy, I'm afraid I'm not a tenant here. I *own* Mon Abri.'

'But that's impossible! I own it, or at least I shall when the will's been sorted out.' She had spoken hastily, but stopped herself as the import of his words struck home. He certainly couldn't own it. But he had spoken as if he believed he did. Oh, no! This was even worse! Nick had obviously been conned—probably to the tune of thousands and thousands of francs, and *she* was going to have to be the one to spell it out to him.

'I'm afraid it wasn't Jean-Claude's to sell,' she added sympathetically. 'I know this must be an awful shock for you——'

'I didn't buy it from Jean-Claude, Lizzy. I bought it from an Englishman by the name of James Colby.'

'Grandpa!' Lizzy's jaw dropped. The information hit her like a thunderbolt. Suddenly her mouth was dry, and her mind dull and uncomprehending.

'Assuming you're the grandchild of James and Hester Colby, then yes.'

'But Grandpa's dead,' she said weakly.

'I'm sorry to hear that. I must say, I very much liked what little I saw of him.'

'But he couldn't have sold you the house! He died over a year ago, and, anyway, it was Grandma's. She left it to me.'

'I'm sorry, Lizzy, but your grandfather was very much alive when I bought Mon Abri from him. Admittedly it was a couple of years ago, and in very unconventional circumstances. But I can assure you that the papers he gave me were in his name. There was no mention of his wife as a joint owner.'

'You mean…' she exclaimed incredulously '…oh, this is absurd. I can't believe it!' Her face was burning, and she had to swallow hard to avoid choking on her words. 'You mean to say,' she began again, 'you're telling me that you think you own this place?'

'As it happens I can——'

But she was no longer listening. She sat very still, her eyes blankly registering his moving lips.

'Now look here,' she said fiercely, as the wheels of her mind began to grind into life again, 'this is crazy. This is my *home*. I've just inherited it. Grandma wanted *me* to have it. It was hers first and then she left it to me. She loved me and I loved her. That's why she wanted me to have it.' She flashed him an accusing look. 'So it can't possibly be yours. You've been tricked in some way. I'm very sorry for you, but the house is mine!'

He had been quite controlled throughout her outburst, surveying her in grave silence, his hands folded loosely in his lap.

For a fleeting second she wanted to reach across the table and shake him very hard. But he looked as immovable as a rock. It would be pointless. Oh, how could he be so calm? He looked so sure of himself. He should be the one panicking—losing his temper—not her! A huge well of self-pity opened up inside her to replace the burned-out fury. She wanted to open her mouth wide, like a child, and howl. But of course she couldn't. She was grown-up, and feeling sorry for herself was going to be of no practical use at all. Anyway, crying might make him feel sorry for her. She winced at the thought.

He was waiting sombrely for her anger to pass. She chewed at the corner of her mouth, wishing he would be the one to break the silence. But he didn't. He just went on sitting there, his grey eyes watching her unemotionally while she struggled to regain her composure, and the colour faded from her cheeks.

At last she muttered resignedly, 'I'm sorry. I shouldn't have lost my temper like that.'

'That's OK,' he said reassuringly. And then, surprisingly, his face broke into a smile, deep lines carving themselves from cheekbone to jaw, where, as a boy, his dimples would have been.

'Let me pour you some more wine,' he suggested, filling her glass before she had time to protest. 'You mustn't let these little setbacks spoil your enjoyment of the finer things of life, you know?' And again that tormenting smile flashed across his features. 'Now drink up and then we can sort out what's to become of you.'

So much for her efforts to calm herself down! That last remark set her teeth on edge. She glowered furiously. It couldn't possibly be that simple! Oh, dear me... There's been a bit of a mistake... Sorry, Lizzy... Never mind... Have a glass of wine... Her gorge rose mutinously at his assumption that with a few brief words the matter could be settled for all time.

'So what were those unconventional circumstances, then?' she asked challengingly, feeling ready to take up the cudgels again and crack his sickening complacency.

Nick eased himself back in his chair, and sipped from his glass before explaining.

'We met in a hotel bar in Beirut, your grandfather and I,' he began. 'I was still in journalism then. He was a sort of vagabond prince, travelling the world on a shoestring. One of those extraordinary characters who fetch up in places like that. We got to talking. He told me that he'd reached a stage in his journey where he badly needed cash to fulfil his dreams.'

'To find the bird of paradise...' whispered Lizzy bitterly, beginning to believe his story. There couldn't be two men like that in the world.

Nick offered her a brief smile of recognition. 'That's right. Anyway, I needed a retreat to write a novel I'd been brewing for some time. We demolished a bottle of Scotch between us that night. By the time the bottle was empty we'd decided to exchange our assets—in his case the ownership of Mon Abri; in mine, the contents of my bank account—and follow our respective stars. We drew up a rough contract there and then. We did what we could to make sure it was watertight, even though it was highly unconventional.' An amused smile played about his mouth at the recollection.

'I'm glad you find it funny,' said Lizzy sourly. 'You do realise that the house wasn't his to sell?'

Nick's face lost its animation. 'That's not the way he told it, Lizzy. And I believed him. I liked your grandfather enormously. He was a unique character. The memory of him always brings a smile to my face. I'm certainly sorry that he didn't live to fulfil all those crazy dreams of his.'

Lizzy bit her lip and blinked hard against the sting of tears. She wasn't about to argue with that. Grandpa had always amused her too. It was comforting to know that there was someone else in the world who remembered him with affection.

A sick knot was weaving itself in the pit of her stomach. She pushed away her untouched glass of wine, and closed her eyes. So Grandpa had taken the deeds of Mon Abri with him when he'd disappeared? And the time had come when he'd needed the money. No doubt it would have cost a lot to finance his trip to the Antipodes. Anyway, it seemed that Nick did, after all, have some sort of legitimate claim on the house, even if it was rather tenuous. But where did that leave her? Perhaps she should have taken her foot off the brake after all, leapt clear, pushed the van over the precipice and declared bankruptcy?

A picture of her mother's face, blinking very fast as she always did when she was warning Lizzy against the perils of her impetuosity, and pursing her small mouth, flashed across her mind. It jolted her out of her misery.

She opened her eyes and gave him as brisk a smile as she could manage. 'You wouldn't like to marry me, would you?' she asked drily.

His features resolved themselves into a puzzled frown. 'Marry you?'

'Yes,' she sighed, with a half-hearted laugh. 'You see, my mother warned me against coming out here to start up my business. She said I'd be bound to fail and she couldn't bear the idea of the family name being dragged through the bankruptcy courts.'

She sighed again. '*Braithewaite*. She always says it as if everybody should recognise it—as if it were one of the names of the great aristocratic families of England, when in reality there are hundreds and hundreds of us in the phone book! Anyway, with bankruptcy staring me in the face it looks as if I'd better change my name fast, or, according to my mother at any rate, my father will have a heart attack.'

His eyes narrowed engagingly. Then he laughed. This time, though, she didn't join him. It was all far too dispiriting. Though she still didn't see how Grandpa could have sold the house without Grandma's consent. Or, at least, not legally. Anyway, surely he would have told her about the sale once he arrived home? They were so close, despite Grandpa's unorthodox departures to go bird-watching in far-flung corners of the globe. They had been together constantly for the six months before he died. He would undoubtedly have told her, and she would certainly have changed her will accordingly. After all, she was always changing her will. It was one of her major hobbies once she got too weak to do her gardening. Perhaps there *was* a chance, after all?

'We'll have to get the lawyers to sort all this out,' she said at last.

He shook his head doubtfully, but said nothing.

'After all, that contract of yours sounds pretty dubious.'

'Er—well, perhaps... Though as I said——'

'I don't expect you to say anything which might incriminate your precious contract,' she said spiritedly, finding her confidence unexpectedly reviving. She reached out a hand and drew her wine glass back towards her. 'But I shan't go down without a fight, you know?'

'I didn't imagine,' he said, running his tongue over his lips, 'for one single moment that you would.'

CHAPTER TWO

WHILE Lizzy's brain was positively whirling, trying to sort out the implications of Nick's devastating revelations, her body was betraying signs of exhaustion. She yawned and stretched hugely several times, muttering a muffled apology from the midst of a spectacularly wide yawn.

'You've obviously had a tiring journey,' commented Nick in response. 'Perhaps you'd better go to bed. You can take the guest-room. We can sort things out properly in the morning.'

'Guest-room!' She knew he hadn't meant to be offensive, but the notion of being a *guest* stung so sharply that she was positively scalded with anger. 'You mean that poky room at the end of the landing next to the linen store? I was planning to use that room for packaging my goods! This is my house, you know, until you manage to prove otherwise.'

At last he responded with something less than equanimity. 'Yes,' he said roughly, 'I do mean the guest-room. You'll find that it's undergone quite a transformation. The linen store is an en-suite shower-room now. You'll be quite comfortable as a guest in my house.'

'It's quite all right,' she replied obstinately. 'I shall make myself a little home in the outhouses. I'm planning to use the big one for my pottery, but I can quite easily make up a bed in the smaller one and——'

He made a dismissive clicking noise with his tongue. It was quite clear she was making no impact on him at all, no matter how forcefully she expressed herself. For all his calm exterior he was clearly not open to negotiation. That knowledge simply strengthened Lizzy's resolve.

'This is absurd,' he said coldly. 'I accept that you'll need to consult a lawyer before you're prepared to give up your claim to Mon Abri. But it isn't your house and you can't live here. My offer of a room for the night is quite civilised under the circumstances. Why not accept it with a good grace instead of making ridiculous noises about camping in the outhouse?'

His scathing manner riled her afresh. 'This *is* my house and I shall sleep where I choose...' she said fiercely, and, tossing her mass of curls back over her shoulders, she strode off around the side of the house to find her new home.

When she returned a few moments later, her face was burning with fury and she wasn't so much striding as stomping. 'My bedroom and workshop are both stacked floor to ceiling with sacks of something. I'd be grateful if you could move them for me.' She folded her arms briskly across her chest, as if to signify that she meant business.

His grey eyes assumed a cool distance. 'It's animal feed,' he said. 'Pig nuts, to be exact. I'm letting one of the local farmers use the outhouses as a feed-store. If I'd had prior notice of your booking I could have made other arrangements, but as it is——'

'Then I'll move them myself,' she said, her green eyes wide and challenging.

He got lazily to his feet and caught one of her wrists in his broad hand. 'Lizzy,' he said firmly, 'you'll do no such thing...'

If she hadn't had her arms folded his fingers wouldn't have brushed lightly against her breast. The feathery accidental touch had the alarming effect of a static shock on her skin, making all the fine hairs on her body stand to attention. Her nipples followed suit. She hugged her folded arms even closer, her anger turned inwards now on her own alarming response. She prayed that he wouldn't notice.

But he already had. His eyes travelled to his hand which had registered the tightening of her muscles under his touch. They came to rest briefly on the urgent peaks, pushing tellingly against the clinging fabric of her T-shirt. His eyebrows rose questioningly.

'Well, well...' he said softly. The beginnings of a smile gathered around his eyes.

'How dare you...?' Her voice quavered dangerously, and she swallowed hard against the dryness of her throat. 'Let go of my arm!'

Slowly, deliberately, he uncurled his fingers and let go of her wrist. His eyes had hardened again into brittle mirrors which showed her nothing but her own reflection.

'The sacks,' he said in a voice which had become palpably harsher, thicker, 'will spoil if they aren't properly stored. The man to whom they belong is very poor. He's trying to diversify his meagre farming interests to help provide for his family. If you spoil his feed his animals—and eventually his family—will suffer. So you can forget any fey ideas about the gypsy life and either stay in the house or drive back to Albi and find yourself accommodation there.'

'I'm not going,' she muttered, her face burning furiously. 'And I'm not going tomorrow or the next day or the next. I'm setting up a pottery here, one way or another. And what's more, I've already done it...'

He frowned suspiciously, his lips a hard, resistant line. 'Already done it?'

'Yes. I've got several thousand printed letters, with this address at the top. And banks in England and France have business accounts in my name at this address. And I've made arrangements with a parcel delivery service, and suppliers to collect and deliver here. And...' she fumbled in her shoulder-bag for a carefully folded piece of newspaper '...look!' She held the sheet of newsprint out to him at arm's length.

He came forward and flicked it from her fingers. He started to read aloud, in a voice thick with sarcasm. '"The Lady of the Flowers terracotta wall-planter... Suitable for outdoor use or conservatories. When planted with trailing greenery, this exquisitely modelled girl's head will make a stunning feature of even the dreariest..."' He stopped, briefly scanned the rest of the advertisement, and then allowed his eyes scour her.

'You mean to tell me these adverts have already appeared in English newspapers? You're running a mail-order business from my *home*?'

She nodded, keeping her head high. 'Why not? I had every right to do what I liked with my own house, surely?'

'I'll forward your mail,' he responded curtly. 'You'll just have to undo all your hard work, and re-do it again from some other premises.'

Lizzy held the tip of her tongue grimly between her teeth. This was all proving remarkably difficult to explain. The trouble was that, whoever should ultimately prove to be the true owner of Mon Abri, for the time being at least he had the upper hand. It was his furniture in the rooms, his food in the larder, his hot water in the pipes. Possession, she remembered having heard it said, was nine points of the law... And yet it was quite impossible for her to give in.

'I can't change the address,' she explained miserably, struggling to master her emotions and bring the discussion back on to a reasonable footing. Some of the heat seeped from her face. 'I've signed a contract. If I change my address I'll forfeit everything...'

She thought his dark eyebrows might actually disappear into his hairline, so high did they shoot at this remark.

'You mean you're *under contract* to work from here...?' His voice was laced with disbelief.

'Yes.'

He folded his arms across his chest, and leaned back against the balustrade which bordered the terrace. 'I'm waiting...' he said, a thin thread of danger underlining his words.

Damn. Those forearms of his, in all their muscular, sun-bronzed glory, were directly in her line of vision. What a stupid time to be distracted by something like that! She forced her eyes to concentrate on his face. That was not much better. The high forehead, the piercing grey eyes, the blunt features and the strong curves of his mouth were all just as annoyingly compelling. She gratefully settled her gaze on the shimmering line of the mountains folding away into the distance.

'I've signed an advertising contract with the *Sunday Recorder*,' she began uneasily.

It was no good. One way or another she was going to have to explain it all. And the sooner she got on with it the better. She took a deep breath. 'I've taken out a run of mail-order ads in their new "Craft Workshop" supplement. They had a special offer for people who signed up for the first issue and guaranteed to run their ads completely unchanged for six months. It was a bargain.'

'What sort of a bargain?' His eyes had narrowed assessingly.

'Half price. And half of eight and a half thousand pounds is still an awful lot of thousands. So you see, I can't afford to break the contract by changing my address. If I do, they'll scrap the rest of the run. Which at present would mean twenty-five of the twenty-six ads I've paid for. I've sold everything. My bits of furniture, my car...everything, just to get started. I can't afford to pay for another lot of ads. I can't even afford to transport the van back to England. So you see...' she tailed off, shrugging her shoulders fatalistically '...I've got to stay here. Whether you like it or not.'

He shook his head slowly, fixing her hard with his steely gaze. 'Nearby, maybe. But not here. Even then I've got six months of hassle, re-routing mail and phone calls and deliveries and God knows what else. And all just because *you* couldn't resist a bargain!'

'Not phone calls...' she muttered. 'I didn't get round to arranging to have a phone installed...I was going to do that this week some time...'

His expressive brows dismissed her protest as being unworthy of his comment. 'None the less, I've got six months of interruptions when I'm trying to get my *own* work done, just because you get greedy when you see a bargain. You should have waited for the July sales and bought yourself a dress. It would have been a damn sight cheaper.'

Lizzy struggled to hang on to her hard-won composure. She hardly ever bought clothes in the sales! She knew it was just a throw-away remark, designed to belittle her, but she resented it badly. After all, she hadn't meant any of this to happen when she had laid her plans.

'I didn't do all this just to inconvenience you!' she exclaimed defensively. 'It's hardly my fault that you were stupid enough to buy a house from someone who had no right to sell it to you. And when you were drunk, at that! I have merely taken advantage of an unrepeatable offer which will enable me to offer my wares to thousands of potential customers every week, without having all the problems of trying to find a shop to display my planters for me.'

'You should have taken a job selling advertising. You've obviously swallowed the sales pitch hook, line and sinker.'

'I did no such thing! I'm not that gullible. Look, I spent nearly a year after art school struggling to sell my work. By the time I found a shop prepared to take a gamble, and then priced things so that the retail markup didn't make them too expensive, there was no time to make the wretched things, and no profit left to live on. All craft workers have the same selling problems. That's why the supplement was launched. To fill a hole in the market . . .'

'To line the pockets of the newspaper owners, more like. I used to be a journalist. I know how these things work.'

'But you don't know how hard it is making a living as a potter, do you? If my planters don't sell, and the newspaper is the only one to profit, well, at least I've given it a try. And if it does work . . . then it will have been worth every penny of the expense. Anyway, it's none of your business how I choose to spend my money. Or live my life, come to that!'

He let out a low, throaty growl, and lifted the palms of his hands to his jaw, rubbing them raspingly over the dark shadow of his chin. It was as if he was trying to rub away her infuriating presence with the gesture.

'You *aren't* staying here,' he said suddenly with an unexpected vehemence.

She had realised that already. Unfortunately, *he* didn't know that he was talking to someone who had extensive experience of being thwarted. Persistence, she knew perfectly well, would not pay off when faced with such resolute implacability. But it always made *her* feel a whole lot better to battle on to the bitter end. Had he known, she thought wryly, he might have clammed up and let her get on with it. It would have saved a lot of time.

'Sorry, but I have to,' she insisted, placing her hands defiantly on her hips.

'You can get premises in Albi. I'll forward your mail. You needn't tell the *Recorder* about your change of address. They're hardly likely to send out a roving reporter to investigate, anyway. Rents aren't too bad in town, and I'll lend you——'

'Absolutely not!' Lizzy was quite taken aback by the force with which the exclamation sprang from her lips. She felt her face colour deeply yet again. 'I'm quite self-sufficient, thank you. I wouldn't dream of taking a penny of your money. Nor of using you as an unpaid messenger while I practise a risky deceit. I shan't get in your way. But I shan't go, either.'

He glared at her determinedly. 'Won't get in my way?' he echoed, his voice sounding truly appalled. 'Don't go making promises you can't keep, Elizabeth *Braithewaite*! I've a deadline to meet, and I'm damned if I'm going to tolerate a distraction like...like you!'

Her pride was urging her to get back into the van and disappear for however many months it took for her ownership of the house to be legally established. But if she did that her advertising contract would be void and she could kiss goodbye to her dreams of having her own ceramics workshop forever. Anyway, she had nowhere in the world to run to. And Grandma had wanted her to live here. She just *had* to stand her ground.

He turned his back on her before speaking again.

'Right now you have a choice. You can either get up to the guest-room and out of my sight, or take that ugly old van of yours off into the wide blue yonder,' he ordered, his voice low and dangerous. 'Because I'm not prepared to discuss this any further.'

He was right. The room was no longer poky, but attractively furnished and decorated in a simple country style. After hovering hesitantly for a few moments, Lizzy had decided that there was no better way of asserting her rights to the house than by marching into it and taking up residence. Even if the outhouses had been empty, it might have weakened her position if she had insisted on living out there like some pathetic poor relation. Turning on her heel also had the welcome effect of hiding from him the tell-tale glimmer of tears, welling unbidden in her eyes.

After a luxurious shower the bed looked wonderfully inviting, and it wasn't long before she was stretched out exhausted between the starched cotton sheets, her hair splayed across the pillow. She didn't for one moment believe that she would sleep a wink—she had far too much on her mind for that. But the comfort of lying in a proper bed was attraction enough, after a night on the ferry followed by the next in the van.

So it was with some surprise that she opened her eyes the following morning, to discover that she had slept soundly from the moment her head hit the pillow. She felt refreshed and cheerful, and slightly alarmed by the quality of light which seeped around the edge of the curtains. A glance at her watch confirmed that it was well after ten. Considering the absurdly early hour at which she had retired it was no wonder she felt so splendidly wide awake. She hastily leapt from her bed and rushed into the little bathroom to clean her teeth.

He must have heard her moving about, because within a few minutes he rapped loudly on her door.

'Lizzy? Make sure you're decent. I'm coming in...'

'Just a mo...' she called, hurriedly donning her white brodcrie anglaise wrap and scrambling to open the curtains before the door opened.

He brought a tray, laden with coffee and croissants, butter and apricot jam, and a bulging carrier bag which he propped against the foot of the bed.

'Breakfast,' he announced drily. 'I hope everything is to your satisfaction.' His voice had lost the cutting edge it had acquired the previous evening. Thank goodness. And he was wearing a shirt in a cool blue cotton, with the sleeves fastened at the wrist. Also thank goodness. If the events of the previous day had yet to tangle themselves around Lizzy's busy brain, at least she had not forgotten the weird affect on her psyche of the mere sight of his naked forearms. She was determined to cope with the problems of her enforced residence in his—or should that be her?—house. But she'd rather not have to look at his arms while she did so.

'Thanks. This is very kind of you. I'm sorry I slept so late...'

He shrugged. 'Actually, the breakfast is just an excuse.' He picked up the carrier bag and tumbled the contents out on to the bed. 'What I really wanted to see you about was...this!'

She stared in open-mouthed astonishment at the pile of letters lying on the bed.

'Oh...' Her mouth dropped open at the sight of the huge heap of mail. She tore open an envelope. A cheque fluttered out, accompanied by a letter and a coupon clipped from a newspaper. She opened several more. The contents were identical.

He was leaning nonchalantly against the wall, his eyes coolly appraising.

Since she had awoken she had thought of nothing but him, one way and another. She had bridled once or twice at the memory of his harsh refusal to let her stay, and had burned with embarrassment as she recalled her own fierce assertiveness. She had soon discovered that there was a granite core masked by that superficial ease of his. Apart from that she had managed to figure out nothing at all about him. Except that she had about as little impact upon him as a gnat. Correction—a gnat bite could cause quite a nasty irritation. She doubted she rated that high in his estimation.

But in none of the memories had his physical presence intruded in the way it did now. She was painfully conscious of his bulk, propped against the wall, watching her as she opened her mail. She had quite forgotten how attractive he was... quite forgotten the prickling excitement that stirred inside her at the mere sight of him. Quite forgotten how difficult it had been to keep her eyes from being endlessly drawn to him.

'They're orders...' she said with a bright smile, as if that explained everything.

He inhaled deeply, so that his chest swelled visibly beneath the soft blue cotton of his shirt. When he let his breath out it was with an exasperated hiss.

'So is this the quantity of mail I can expect to have to deal with every day for the next six months?'

Her green eyes opened wide. 'I don't know. I shouldn't think so. I would imagine that this is just sort of... beginner's luck...'

'But I thought advertising was supposed to have a cumulative effect? The more you advertised, the more you sold...'

'Yes...' she said vaguely, watching her own hands gather together the envelopes and beginning to count them. 'The sales rep said something of the sort, too. But I'm not sure that it can be right. After all, people will either like the planters and decide to buy one, or they won't. It's not as if my adverts are trying to persuade them or anything. Is it?'

'Who knows?' He shrugged. 'All I know is that I have no intention of spending the next six months re-addressing envelopes——'

'But you won't have to!' she exclaimed, with what she hoped was artless ingenuity. She really didn't want to start quarrelling again, before the day had even properly begun! 'After all, *I'll* be here to pick up my own mail.'

He scowled furiously. Unfortunately, it didn't mar his appeal one little bit. She found her hands clutching at the lapels of her dressing-gown, drawing it tighter across her breasts. She had always thought it very demure, concealing her as it did from neck to toe. But suddenly she was alarmingly aware of her own nakedness beneath it.

'I thought I made myself plain last night, but if I'm forced to repeat——'

'There's no need to say anything again,' she butted in sharply, anxious to get the conversation over with as quickly as possible. 'I understood you perfectly well. But I also made myself plain. Can we please avoid going over the same old ground again?'

'You are wasting your breath, Lizzy Braithewaite, if you think you can persuade me to give in.'

'I don't think there should be any question of either of us giving in. We both have good reason to feel that we own the house, and that we have every right to be here. The law will make the final decision. But until it does, I think you should respect my feelings in the same way that I'm respecting yours.'

He snorted disparagingly. 'That's just a roundabout way of saying that I should let you stay in my house!'

'No, it's not! I don't want you to *let* me stay in *your* house. That makes it sound as if I'm your guest. I have no intention of sponging off you or intruding upon your life at all. I simply ask to be left in peace to live in my house, which also happens, for the time being at any rate, to be your house as well.'

'Semantics!'

She shook her head. 'It's not just a question of the definition of words,' she asserted stoutly. 'It's more than that. It's a question of feelings—of attitudes—of how

we handle a situation which is potentially very uncomfortable for both of us.'

For the first time since she had lost her temper the
previous evening he looked at her with a keener edge.

Then he shrugged. 'Even so,' he said dismissively, 'I've
been used to thinking of this place as my own. I need
my solitude in order to work. For heaven's sake, that's
why I bought this house in the first place! An ar-
rangement like that would be easy for you. But it's out
of the question as far as I'm concerned.'

'Easy? When I'm sleeping in a bed you bought, in a
room you decorated, and washing in water heated by the
boiler you had installed? You must be joking! I have to
remind myself every second that this is *my* place and I
have every right to be here. But,' she continued breezily,
'I'm working hard on it. So don't think for one minute
that I'll turn tail and flee. If you want me out you'll
have to get the police to come and carry me away. And
to do that you'd need to prove that I had no right to be
here in the first place...'

His jaw was tightly clenched, and his eyes rock hard.
'No!' His voice was adamant.

For a moment she nearly weakened.

Until he added coldly, 'You wouldn't have any of these
problems if only you'd waited to find out more before
you set off. I'm not paying the price of your stupid
impetuosity.'

The accusation was hardly new. And yet nothing had
ever felt less like a spur-of-the-moment decision. When
she'd heard that Grandma had left her Mon Abri unexpected tears of relief had welled up in her eyes. She
had truly believed herself to be happy until that moment.
But when she had taken in the news, she knew she'd

been waiting all her life for that sense of completeness . . . That feeling of having a home to go to at last. There was nothing to hold her . . . nothing to stop her . . . and nothing, but nothing, was going to send her scurrying back. She would pitch a tent in the garden if need be!

'I'll use the garage for my workshop,' she announced, fighting to keep the tremor out of her voice. 'And I'll spend my time either there or in this room. And I'll contribute half towards all the domestic bills. But I won't go.'

He eyed her with something approaching scorn. 'Now come on, Cinders,' he muttered caustically. 'Only yesterday you were busy pleading poverty . . .'

Triumphantly she picked up the stack of envelopes, and waved them in front of his face. 'That,' she said firmly, 'was yesterday. Today I have fifty-seven orders.' And she let her eyes rest briefly and with enormous pride on the evidence of her success. 'Cinders . . .' she added huskily '. . . has turned into a princess. So if you have no more objections, perhaps we can consider the matter settled?'

And then he did a very surprising thing. He laughed. He laughed with that same dry, humorous note with which he had greeted her assumption that he was French.

Then he said, 'But you can't have turned into a princess, yet. After all, you haven't been kissed by a frog. Though perhaps, as I've got French arms, this might suffice.' And he leaned across and gave her a brusque peck on the cheek.

It was totally unexpected. And it was supposed to make *her* laugh. She knew *that*, for goodness' sake. But the fragile touch of his lips on her cheek, the rough masculinity of his newly shaved chin brushing against her skin, set that electrical charge crackling again so that she was effectively silenced. She felt her skin clinging tight and she knew that a pink blush had raced to her cheeks. So much for long sleeves!

She had obviously embarrassed him by her failure to laugh, because when she dared to look up he was gazing out of the window, his shoulders hunched in an attitude of extreme annoyance, his features unreadable.

She tugged her thin cotton wrap closer around herself as she shivered slightly. He must be generating frost, because the sunlight streaming in through the window was warm enough.

He turned abruptly and opened the door. But before he went he muttered, 'I'll clear out the garage for you. I'm damned if I'm letting you anywhere near my car after seeing how you handled that van.'

Before she could reply he had gone.

She was astonished that the battle had been won. And pleased too, of course. But she was alarmed by the way he had seemed to register—twice now—her overtly sexual response to the briefest meeting of their flesh. It was as if the integrity of his exterior had cracked—leaving something more...raw exposed. Was that why he had so abruptly and surprisingly changed his mind? Because he'd sensed the powerful effect he had on her? Did he think her presence might have its compensations after all? She didn't want to give him the wrong idea. She certainly wasn't interested in becoming involved with him. She wasn't even interested in something more light-hearted—more innocuous—than that.

Anna had once accused her of cutting off her nose to spite her face where men were concerned. 'Just because you're determined never to marry oughtn't mean that you can't have the occasional romance, just for fun.'

The trouble was, Lizzy had reflected sadly, that was exactly what it did mean. She knew she wasn't yet capable of having casual affairs. Later, perhaps, when she was a mature and successful artist, with a weathered face and rusty hair, she might take a lover. One who brought frail bunches of violets to her door in the evenings, and who talked about art and literature and made love to her—though she was a little vague about the details on this point as she had kept both of her serious boyfriends from student days very much at arm's length. Anyway, this mystery lover would be very passionate, but in the morning he would depart to resume his own life, leaving her to lose her temper and make her pots and read her library books in her own peculiarly intense and infuriating way, without driving him mad.

Yes, later, when she had mellowed with age, such a thing might be possible. But she knew that she still cherished too many of her youthful romantic illusions for it to work for her now.

CHAPTER THREE

LIZZY set aside the flowery sundress she had laid out ready, and dressed herself instead in denim shorts and an over-sized white T-shirt. Then she plaited her hair severely, and plonked her battered sunhat in place to shield her nose. Not being a distraction couldn't start soon enough as far as she was concerned.

He wasn't clearing the garage, after all, but working. She could hear the spasmodic rattle of his typewriter issuing in short bursts from one of the upstairs rooms. In fact the garage was locked, and she decided it would be reneging on their deal if she were to disturb him for the key. She had plenty, after all, to keep her busy.

He appeared at lunchtime, looking pensive.

'Hi!' he greeted her casually. 'Come and have something to eat.'

'Er—no, thanks. I've been down to the village and bought some food. I'll take it up——'

'Oh, don't be so absurd!' he interrupted briskly. 'I've already told Madame Roget to prepare lunch for two. She'll be bringing it out in a moment. Sit down.' And he gestured briskly towards one of the rattan chairs.

To her annoyance she found herself obeying orders. 'We must sort out the financial arrangements,' she muttered.

'I'll bill you,' he responded drily. 'Complete with a ten-per-cent service charge.'

43

She couldn't help smiling. 'Don't joke about it. It's important to me. Honestly. I don't want to impose.'

He shrugged vaguely. 'You're not. Or at least, not at the moment. I invited you to eat with me, after all. When you get on my nerves I'll let you know.'

'Thanks.' It was her turn to offer a dry smile. But he didn't seem to notice. There was something withdrawn and distant in his manner which suggested that he was only half aware of her presence.

'What sort of novels do you write?' she continued, anxious to re-establish their relationship on an easier basis.

'I try to write good ones,' he said.

She waited for him to continue, but he simply began to drum his fingers impatiently on the table.

Fortunately Madame Roget appeared at that moment with the food. It was a simple meal of cooked meats and salad, served with ice-cold water laced with slivers of lime, and accompanied by an overflowing bowl of fruit.

For a while the business of helping themselves to the food and eating took over from conversation. She tried asking him a few questions about his days in journalism. But, though he answered politely enough, he kept his comments brief. There was a spareness of speech, almost amounting to an evasiveness, which warned her not to ask too much—although superficially he was pleasant enough. But at least there was no sign of the anger which had surfaced at their previous encounters.

The simple lunch was quite delicious. The view down into the rugged valley was soothing and inspiring at the same time. The view across the table—those sunburned arms, that high forehead, those cropped, almost black curls and the wry smile—was anything but soothing.

Lizzy had to keep dragging her gaze back to the gardens...the mountains...anywhere that wouldn't reveal how compellingly she was drawn to him.

As Nick reached out to take a nectarine from the bowl, he suddenly looked up at her with a new animation in his eyes.

'Tell me about this grandfather of yours,' he said, with what sounded like a genuine curiosity. 'The old man fascinated me. I'd like to know more.'

It was easy to tell that Nick had been a journalist. He had a way of asking questions which made you feel he was really interested in the answers. It wasn't long before Lizzy had been led far beyond her childhood memories of Grandpa. Soon she was spilling out the tale of her struggle to earn a place on one of the best ceramics courses in the country, to be a first-rate student, and to earn her living from her work before resigning herself to two years of dreary office routine.

'But you were a graduate? Surely you could have found something more interesting to do than that?'

'Yes. But I was spending my evenings and weekends at my wheel. If I'd had a more demanding daytime job I would never have had the energy.'

'And what did your co-workers make of you?'

'What a personal question! To tell you the truth, I think I drove them mad...'

'Ah, now that figures!'

'Don't be rude! It was only my fingernails which drove them mad.'

'Your fingernails?'

'Yes. There were three other women in the office, all very sleek and well-manicured. And a jowly man with a beer-belly and a crude line in sexist remarks and hor-

rible bitten nails. They were all appalled by my nails.'
She laid her long-fingered, deft hands on the table for
him to inspect. 'Oh. They're looking OK at the moment,'
she commented in surprise. 'That's because I haven't
been handling clay for a couple of weeks. Usually they
have to be kept very short so that they don't mark the
clay, and then the wretched stuff gets underneath them
and makes them look dirty no matter how much I scrub.'

He reached out one of his own hands to examine her
nails, but she snatched her hands away and folded them
uneasily in her lap.

'I wasn't going to bite you...' he remarked, his eyes
glittering with amusement.

'I know...' she muttered uncertainly, trying to think
of something to say which would deflect the conversation. She'd behaved like a scalded cat, and didn't want
him asking any of his probing questions about *that*!

With a sudden burst of inspiration she asked, 'Do you
have false teeth?'

'What?'

'Oh, dear. I'm afraid that question didn't come out
the way it was meant to. I didn't think your teeth were
false for one moment. They're very nice teeth. Very realistic...' Oh, lord! What was she saying now? That
runaway tongue of hers was doing it again...

'Thank you,' he said caustically, tugging on a front
tooth to prove its authenticity.

'What I meant to ask was whether you know where
people get their false teeth made around here. I need to
get hold of some top-grade plaster of Paris for making
my moulds, you see, and a dental suppliers is usually
the easiest place to get it. I was just wondering if there
was anywhere in Albi...'

He shrugged. 'I haven't a clue. You may have to go all the way to Montpellier for some of the stuff you need. There's a phone book in the house, though. You can check things out in there.'

She turned back to the list she'd been making earlier, hoping she wasn't blushing beetroot after making that gaffe about his teeth. She had never been unsettled like this before by any man, and she didn't know how to handle it. She added a few notes in her sprawling hand.

'I'll go and clear out the garage for you,' he offered.

She looked up. 'There's no need. Honestly. I can do that myself. All you need to do is unlock it and move the car. I meant it when I said I didn't want to disturb you.'

He winced. 'I think,' he murmured, 'you're going to end up disturbing me whether you mean to or not. Take those legs for a start...'

She pressed her lips into a thin line of disapproval, tucking her legs under her chair. But inside her stomach was churning in an anything but disapproving way. It was bad enough his making a remark of that kind, without her insides reacting to it with such childish glee. Tomorrow, she resolved, she would wear her jeans.

'I'm sorry about my legs. But I need them for moving about. I'm afraid you'll have to put up with them.' Her voice sounded arch—haughty—even to her own ears. She'd made her point, but she didn't want to start another argument. She sighed, and then added more reasonably, 'And I do realise I'm not the easiest of people to be with. But really I *can* see to things myself. Like the garage. Speaking of which... are all those shelves still there?'

'Yes...'

'Oh, good. Great. They'll come in very handy.' She scanned her list, hoping she was creating an illusion of intense concentration.

He pushed back his chair and got to his feet. He took a few steps away from her, then suddenly turned back to give her a quizzical look.

'Lizzy, do you have a photographic memory?'

'No,' she said, looking up at him in surprise, her equilibrium restored by the change of subject. 'But I do have all my own teeth...'

He smiled. 'It's just that you seem to remember so many obscure details about this place. Did you live here when you were a child or something?'

'No...' she said. 'I came here on holiday three times. Twice as a child with both my grandparents, and then for a whole eight weeks with Grandma when I was fourteen.'

'But that must have been ten years ago?'

She nodded. 'Nearly eleven.'

'Then how come you remember the linen store and the fact that there are two outhouses, one big and one small, and all those shelves in the garage? I can't even remember where I went on holiday the year I was fourteen, let alone details like that.'

'No,' she said consideringly. 'Though it's a much longer time since you were fourteen. The mind often goes before the teeth, so I'm told...'

'Seriously, though?'

'Seriously, there's a very straightforward explanation. That last summer I spent the whole eight weeks building a scale model of the house.'

'Oh,' he said, and drifted away to move the car, his mind clearly set at rest by that useless bit of information.

But Lizzy's mind was suddenly anything but at rest. The memory still had the power to revive all those long-ago feelings that she had hoped to have put behind her forever.

By the end of the day Lizzy was exhausted, but the garage was a workshop. When she had finished Nick was fortunately absent, though the clatter of the typewriter could once again be heard, carrying across the still air in fierce bursts.

Now and again she cast admiring glances at the glossy red Range Rover, which was parked alongside her dilapidated van. It was just the sort of vehicle she might come to need on these mountain roads in winter if she was to get her orders dispatched promptly. She would have to start saving to buy a four-wheel-drive. It began to dawn on her that there was going to be more to making this business work than she had naïvely imagined.

Now that she had had a few hours to wander about the place she was increasingly conscious that the house was very much his in spirit. Outside it still looked like the Mon Abri of her memories. Inside it was entirely Nick Holt. How on earth was all this legal hullabaloo ever going to be sorted out fairly?

And yet it had been Grandma's house and she had wanted Lizzy to have it. It would be very disloyal to her memory to turn her back on it. But then again, Grandpa had sold it to Nick. There was a perfectly honest misunderstanding somewhere at the bottom of all this. But if she went to court might it not look as if she was trying to prove that Grandpa was dishonest? That would hardly be doing *his* memory much of a service, would it? So should she leave? Should she let Nick have the house

when her business was established and she could afford
to find herself another home? What then? No. She
couldn't just walk away from Grandma's bequest.
Perhaps, if the house turned out to be hers, she could
repay Nick the money, somehow...?

She growled. Honestly. Those grandparents had caused
enough trouble when they were alive. What with
Grandma's astonishing disregard for others, and
Grandpa running away to sea at the ripe old age of sixty,
they'd caused more trouble than a pair of adolescents.
And still it hadn't stopped! But she needn't go to see a
lawyer for a few days yet. The only thing that mattered
right now was getting the planters made.

He came to call her for dinner a little after nine. He
must have showered and changed because he was now
dressed in comfortable white cotton trousers, with a white
shirt, open and with its tails hanging free. She groaned
inwardly, knowing that she was going to find her eyes
drawn endlessly to the exposed acres of silken skin. Not
that there was much respite when she looked at his face.
She had no way of guessing how much her magnetised
gaze might be giving her away. Having never experienced this sort of attraction before, she had nothing at
all to gauge it by. How long, for instance, did such things
last? She could only pray that it might depart as suddenly as it had come.

They ate on the terrace, though Nick explained that
it was rarely warm enough to eat outside in the evenings
this early in the summer. 'The air,' he volunteered, 'is
exceptionally still at present. There's often a pleasant
breeze in the day. Then it gets cold later on, and I'm
glad to light a fire. But this hot, settled weather seems
to have set in early this year.'

'How British we are,' she mocked, 'talking about the weather.'

His mouth curved with slow precision into an appreciative smile. 'True,' he conceded, letting his eyes roam over her. 'Especially when there are more important things to discuss. Like our relationship.'

She felt shockingly alarmed. 'What do you mean?' she asked suspiciously. Then, quickly, as her mind grasped what he must have been referring to she continued, 'Oh, you mean about money and use of the kitchen and phone and all that? I thought I'd made it plain that I wanted to contribute properly.'

He gave an irritated sigh. 'Yes. Yes. That, too.'

'You keep dismissing it, as if it weren't important,' she protested. 'But it's very important to me. Here I am, eating as your guest again. But I'm not your guest. Anything but. Once I start paying my way I'll feel a whole lot better about everything.'

'You make such heavy weather of it, Lizzy,' he said. 'Madame Roget prepares the evening meal in the mornings when she comes in to clean. She puts it in the oven on a timeswitch. It's no big deal for her to cook enough for two, rather than one.'

She frowned. 'But it still casts me in the role of guest. If I eat her meals then I *must* help pay her wages. Which I will do.'

'Don't be pedantic. I have a good deal more than I need, these days. Both of my published novels have done well, and I've had a generous advance for the current one.'

'Then I'm pleased for you. But I can't see what it has to do with me. Unless,' she added slyly, 'you feel guilty about the house.'

He gave a terse laugh. 'I don't make a habit of wallowing in guilt, Lizzy. I gave your grandfather a fair price for this place.'

She shrugged. 'Guilty or innocent, there's no reason in the world why you should support me.'

'Look, when I came here first, I too had nothing but my dreams. I'd cashed in everything to try and write. I know what it's like. Fortunately my parents were supportive—come Christmas and birthdays they sent over-large cheques saying that they thought I'd like to choose my own present. Mostly I chose bread and cheese. And my brothers used to come for brief holidays, with car-loads of food, and accidentally leave behind unopened tubes of toothpaste and tablets of soap, and once, in winter, a pair of unworn wellingtons in my size. Perhaps I'm just trying to repay a debt?'

So that was why he was being so helpful? By letting her stick around to get her creative dreams off the ground, he was repaying all those people who'd helped him get started. Really, she ought to be pleased. It was much healthier than allowing herself to believe he was doing it because of her own self.

'No,' she insisted. 'Anyway, you're not my family. You only met me yesterday. And you don't owe me anything.'

'Were you as stubborn as this when you were a child?' he asked wryly.

'Yes.' She hated talking about her childhood.

'You must have been a real handful to bring up, in that case?'

'Yes,' she said ruefully. 'I was.'

He couldn't even begin to guess! After Charles, so placid and agreeable, and such a pleasure to raise, her parents had waited a full seven years before producing her, wanting to savour every minute with Charles before repeating the whole delightful experience with their second son. In the event they had a horrible shock. The baby was a girl. Worse... a baby girl with red hair, a mind of her own and colic... Not a bit like Charles. And not a bit like them, either.

'Tell me about *your* childhood,' she said hurriedly, hoping to direct the conversation away from her own background.

Obligingly he began to tell her about his happy boyhood as the fourth of five sons of a country doctor and his wife. As he talked about that distant time Lizzy sensed a new openness in his manner. At last he talked freely and happily about himself, with none of the caution she had sensed in his responses at lunchtime. His eyes sparkled as he described the delights of a youth spent damming streams... climbing trees... attempting to train caterpillars to do circus tricks... fighting with his brothers... He spoke fluently and amusingly, painting a vivid picture of his early life. Until now Lizzy had not stopped to wonder about the books he wrote. With a pleasurable shiver she realised that they were probably very good. Though she couldn't fathom why it should excite her to believe that he must be good at what he did... She must read them for herself and find out.

As the evening drew to a close she reached a hand up to smooth the hair at her temples. She was tired, and her head was aching slightly.

'You've got a headache,' he said astutely.

'Not really. My hair's a bit uncomfortable in this plait, that's all,' she replied evasively. She didn't want him to worry about her. That wasn't part of the deal.

He unfolded his long frame, and came to stand behind her. To her horror he began to unplait her hair. His fingers combed through it, teasing it out into its usual corkscrewing mass. Luckily she wasn't in a position to see his chest between the open edges of the white shirt, or his arms below the rolled sleeves. But the sensation of his fingers lightly massaging her scalp, and then the back of her neck, was exquisitely pleasurable none the less. The headache disappeared instantly. Her skin tingled in that devastating way once more, and she sensed her nipples tighten into firm, expectant buds beneath her T-shirt as she felt his breath siffling through her hair.

'I like your hair loose,' he murmured. 'It's a wonderful colour.'

'It's dark now,' she muttered abruptly. 'It looks much better at night.'

'It's a wonderful colour in daylight, too.'

'You were obviously made to eat your greens as a child,' she responded, folding her arms firmly across her throbbing breasts, and stifling the urge to turn her face towards him.

'What on earth has that got to do with the colour of your hair?'

'Children who are forced to eat cabbage grow up loving carrots,' she said drily, squirming slightly in an attempt to dispel the delicious sensations that streamed through her.

'I love cabbage,' he countered. 'And Titian...'

It was too much! She stood up, ducking away from his fingers. 'For goodness' sake!' she exclaimed with a forced grin. 'Spare me the purple prose about my carroty hair! I've heard it all... Titianesque! Pre-Raphaelite!

People only go over the top with flattery when they're being insincere.'

He was looking at her with an unnerving intensity. Any minute now he was going to contradict her. It was bad enough trying to talk when her body was fuming at being snatched away from the delicate touch of his hands. But if he paid her another compliment she would choke on her reply.

'I'm tired,' she said quickly, turning away. 'I'm off to bed. Goodnight!'

But he took a step towards her, caught her lightly by the shoulders and spun her round. With a swift movement his face came towards hers, and before she had time to protest his mouth was covering hers and he was kissing her. She had no idea that a kiss could stop her dead in her tracks. No idea that the sensation of his firm lips on hers could make her eyes close, her mouth open softly and her bones melt. She had never experienced real desire—desire so strong and animal that it coursed through her veins in a torrent, awaking sharp, sweet responses in her skin...her mouth...her breasts.

His tongue explored hers, and driven by instinct she yielded to its probing, letting her mouth be possessed, and then, intuitively, kissing him back. His hands moved from her shoulders to her hair, so that her head was drawn closer to his, so that she was plundered by the passion of his tongue. It was only when she found her body inching nearer to his, when some atavistic urge drove her against him, moving in his arms so that the tips of her high, firm breasts could be crushed against his hard chest, that she became frightened. What was she doing? This was madness!

Her hands came up to drive between them, to push against him as her head twisted away.

'Stop!' she cried, her words muffled by the nearness of him.

He loosed his hold, letting his hands rest on her shoulders, and looking into her eyes.

'What's the matter? You want this as much as I do...' he said, his voice bruised with desire.

'No...' she said shakily. 'You're wrong.'

He made a low noise of dissent. 'I'm not. You just told me as much with your mouth, your body—and, one way or another, you've been telling me since the moment you arrived...'

'No!' The protest cut sharply through the night air.

'So it's too soon? You would have liked me to wait. But surely you sensed it from the start? What difference will a few days...weeks...make?'

Oh, lord. So he had understood the effect he was having on her? And presumably he thought that this was what she was after? She gave a low groan.

'You *are* wrong,' she muttered, a shiver running through her. 'It's not what I want. It can't be.'

There was a brief silence. 'There's someone back home, isn't there?' he asked drily.

Reluctantly she forced her head to nod its assent, but she could not meet his eyes. Lying—real lying, not just those little half-truths that made the world go round— was foreign territory to Lizzy. But what else could she do? This way he would get the message. Denying the obvious desire he aroused in her was a waste of time. It was something she clearly couldn't hide from him.

His hands left her shoulders, and dropped to his sides. Her downcast eyes glimpsed the corded muscles of his wrists above the clenched fists.

She swallowed noisily. 'Goodnight,' she whispered, and made her way hastily to the stairs. She was oddly disappointed when he made no reply.

The next day Lizzy awoke at dawn to the disturbing recollection of his mouth melting into her own. Grrr... That was not supposed to have happened! She consoled herself that however much he may have believed she wanted it—and however powerfully she might have responded to him—she *hadn't* done anything intentionally to provoke it. Why, she'd been on her way up to bed when he'd practically *forced* her... But with a guilty flush she stamped determinedly on her train of thought at that point.

Certainly he had caught her unprepared. Certainly *he* had been the one to start kissing her, without any of that preliminary ear-nibbling and eye-gazing to warn her of what he had in mind. And when he *had* kissed her it had been with that unspoken, indefinable insistence of his, which seemed to command her obedience no matter how much she might protest. But he had, after all, stopped when she called a halt. She could have pushed him away the instant his lips brushed hers. She could even have slapped him hard across the face. Strangely, her mind bucked alarmingly at that idea.

There was something so...so unyielding, beneath that relaxed, amused exterior of his. She had a silly feeling that had she tried to slap him it would have been *her* fingers which would have ended up stinging from the shock, while the nerves of his skin would have simply chuckled, tormentingly, at her presumption. No. She couldn't blame him. It was *her* body, after all, which had sent out those eager messages, and had responded so unguardedly when their cry was heard.

She hurried herself into her jeans and down to the kitchen to make coffee, forcing herself to stop thinking about Nick. She had work to do, after all. All those orders! In one day she had received more orders than she had ever dared hope for in a week. Thank goodness that big new kiln was due to be delivered today. She had to clear a space in the workshop and then get on with making some more moulds.

But once out in the garage, her hands kneading the clay, her mind kept creeping off to take another look at that kiss. And the mere recollection of it stirred the blood in her veins and set her pulses racing. She had been quite astonished at the fierce urgency of her response the previous night. But already she felt almost familiar with the tingling manifestations of her new-found sexual awareness. So *this* was what all the fuss was about! Lizzy suspected that twenty-four was a very great age indeed at which to first make the acquaintance of one's instinctive drives. For most people, she guessed, it happened much, much sooner.

But her isolated teenage years at boarding-school had precluded even the merest taste of romance, except, of course, vicariously through the novels she had so avidly consumed. By the time she had arrived at college she had been positively starving for her first taste of love.

But, stupidly, naïvely, she had wanted the whole mythical and wonderful concoction in one fell swoop. Her first boyfriend had complained at her lack of interest in his tentative, inexperienced kisses. But Lizzy had been holding back, waiting to fall headlong in love with him before giving herself wholly and completely to his embraces. She waited. He waited. But she never did fall in love, even though he was very good-looking, and awfully kind. In the end he couldn't wait any longer, and called it a day. And he did it, moreover, in terms which were anything but kind.

She sighed. She hadn't needed a psychologist to tell her that it was the emotional void in her life—the pain of having been born to a family which wouldn't... couldn't... offer her the love which should have been hers by right—which had made her so dizzily determined to find her heart's desire as she grew to adulthood.

The second time it happened it was even worse. She'd gone to lots of parties. She'd had lots of dates with lots of men. But only when she was sure she had found the right man had she accepted a second and then a third date. He was going to be the man of her dreams.

This time she worked really hard on the love angle. She'd listened earnestly to everything he said. She took an interest in his work. She even read the same books as him and learned to savour his vegetarian cuisine— despite the indigestibility of the lentils. In short, she did everything possible to encourage that elusive emotion. And she was getting there. She was sure of it. But, while she had been growing love, he had been growing irritated.

Oddly, it had come as something of a relief when he left her. And it was then that she had realised that she had got herself all wrong. She was used to living without love. She had been happy and self-sufficient until she had started searching for Mr Right. She could be just as happy and just as self-sufficient for the rest of her life, as long as she gave love a miss. Her work was the love of her life, and here she was, at last, with her own workshop and a stack of orders to fulfil.

So what was the problem? And why did she feel this unmistakable sexual craving for a man who was never going to be the man of her dreams? She shook her head. She was damned if she was going to let Nick Holt stand between her and the realisation of everything she had worked for. She was going to put the embarrassment of the kiss firmly behind her and just get on with him as if it had never happened. . .

She didn't have to wait long for the opportunity to test her resolution. By the time she was ready for her ten o'clock cup of coffee he was out on the terrace, basking in the sun.

He was leaning back in the chair, his buttocks propped on the edge of the seat, his long, muscular legs stretched out in front of him. The remains of a simple breakfast were scattered across the table. He was wearing a disreputable pair of cut-off jeans today, with an even older shirt, open and loose, and with the sleeves, inevitably, rolled up. His eyes were closed against the kiss of the morning sun on his face, his head tilted back.

'Hi...' he said softly, though his posture had revealed not the slightest awareness of her approach.

'Oh. Hello,' she responded crisply, slightly unnerved. Surely he didn't have X-ray vision, along with all those other attributes of his?

'Sit down...' He raised the fingers of one hand in a relaxed gesture of invitation.

She perched on the edge of the chair opposite. 'Only for a minute. I'm very busy...'

'You told me that yesterday. Tell me something different for a change.'

'But it's true——'

'I don't doubt it. But it's beginning to pall as a topic of conversation. Why don't you tell me about this lover of yours?'

Thank goodness he had his eyes closed. Colour ran into her cheeks to signal her dismay. She was a hopeless liar! Having once embarked upon the lie, she ought really to have prepared her cover story ready for this moment. Instead of which she'd kept pushing it all out of her mind, hoping against hope that he'd never ask.

'Er—he's...um...very nice.'

'Lucky you. So what's his name?'

Oh, help! Name...? Name...? She could only think of one name, and that was Nicholas. And she could hardly use that! With a strangled sigh of relief she remembered another...

'Charles...' she mumbled.

His head rocked forwards very slightly, as if he might have nodded had he been bothered. 'Charles? Isn't that your brother's name too?'

She stifled a groan. 'Yes. But you misheard me. My boyfriend's name isn't Charles. It's—er—Charlton.'

Now his head dropped fractionally backwards. 'And this rather unusual name of his...? Is it his first name or his second?'

'First. His full name is...ah...Charlton Hest——' She hurriedly caught back the word in the nick of time. 'Hesketh,' she completed, with a muffled sigh of relief.

He was silent.

'It's an old family name,' she added for good measure.

'So he comes from an old family, does he?'

'Yes. That's right. Quite a—er—distinguished lineage, actually.'

'Like the *Braithewaites*, eh?' It was most odd. His mouth was relaxed into an even, straight line. The corners were turning neither up nor down. And yet there was an...an *aura* of a smile about him. An invisible, but very sardonic smile.

'Not exactly. No,' she replied stiffly.

'Does he work? Or is he landed gentry of some sort, this Charlton?'

'He works,' she said decisively, struggling to think of a suitable occupation for him. The face of her ghastly brother Charles swam into view, perched atop his pin-striped suit. 'He's something in the City,' she added with satisfaction. 'Something quite high up, as it happens.'

'And is he passionate?' The non-existent smile intensified.

Oh, this was too much! It suddenly occurred to Lizzy that she didn't *have* to continue with this conversation. Not if he was going to ask questions like that, anyway!

'Very!' she snapped, pushing her chair backwards with a loud scraping sound. She got to her feet. 'Now, if you'll excuse me, I have work to do.'

He didn't respond. He didn't even lift his fingers in a farewell salute.

She glared at him. He still hadn't moved. And his features were still utterly expressionless. The only sound to be heard was the faint rustle of leaves in the light breeze. But for some reason she was absolutely sure that he was laughing.

CHAPTER FOUR

THE postman brought another large bundle of orders that day and the next. And the next. Being busy turned out to be a conversation-killer in more ways than one. There was no time to talk. No time to *breathe*, practically. Before she had set off Lizzy had worked out that she could survive at starvation level on ten orders a week. On twenty she could eat. On thirty she could eat and smile. On forty she could eat, smile, keep the van on the road and buy her favourite hair conditioner. On fifty she could afford to thumb her nose at everyone who'd tried to pour cold water on her plans.

In theory she was going to be able to bathe in hair conditioner and live like a princess. Except that there was no time. And anyway, she doubted whether many princesses spent their days spattered in liquid mud, their nails clipped short and the brims of their sun-hats pulled down against the baking sun. She even ate on the hoof. She bought baguettes and butter and plenty of the pungent Roquefort cheese of the locality, washing it down with Perrier water. The only respite came on her trips into Albi in the van to collect supplies or visit the bank. Her dream was beginning to turn into a nightmare.

Most days Nick would stroll out and watch her working for a while. She would keep her head down, concentrating on rolling out the clay or pressing it dextrously into the moulds. He always looked supremely at ease, looking into the garage, propping one broad shoulder against the door-jamb, while he scrutinised her drily. He rarely spoke.

She hated it when he appeared like that. She hated it because it brought a thrill of pleasure coursing through her veins, tying her stomach in knots, and making her usually deft fingers tremble slightly beneath the onslaught of his indecipherable regard.

He arrived one day with a fresh pile of mail for her. She set it to one side. There was no longer any thrill in opening orders. In fact, she was beginning to pray for a postal strike. She was working from dawn till ten at night as it was, and her leisure activities consisted entirely of washing and sleeping.

'Don't you get bored, making the same things all the time?' he queried, tracing the profile of one of the terracotta faces with his fingertip.

Thank goodness he wasn't doing that to her! She suppressed a delicious shiver. 'Yes,' she agreed, forcing herself to grin cheerfully. 'Of course.'

He looked at her assessingly before wandering over to examine the kiln. 'When are you going to fire all these?'

'Don't worry. I'll read the electricity meter before I do any firing, and pay you whatever it costs. But these heads only need to go in for a relatively short time. It means they'll be slightly porous, but that's ideal considering they'll be filled with damp compost and planted with trailing greenery and nasturtiums and so on.'

He looked across at her. 'They're beautiful just like this. But they must look superb when they have ivy-leafed "hair" tumbling out of them.'

'Thanks.' She let herself smile again, then steeled herself to wander over to join him. Talking about work was pretty safe, after all. 'But the best bit is the flowers.

Look...' And she showed him the clever design features which allowed flowers to be planted so that they formed a coronet over the verdant hair, and a garland around the elegant sweep of the neck.

Nick was generous with his admiration, then asked, 'So why did you transport this hefty wheel all the way to the South of France?'

'For my real work, of course. These planters are my bread and butter. But what I want is to be able to spend part of my time making individual pieces which will all be glazed and fired several times. And which I'll have terrible trouble selling.'

'Oh. I see.' He sounded inexplicably pleased about something. 'And when will you have stock-piled enough planters to be able to get on with your own stuff?'

'Never,' she muttered with a resigned laugh. 'I'm barely keeping up with the orders as it is. Still, I'm getting faster all the time, and the first rush should die back soon.'

He grimaced. 'And if it doesn't?'

'Then I'll just have to work very hard for six months.' She tried to keep a note of buoyant optimism in her voice. Things were bound to work out. It was unthinkable for them not to.

'So all this stuff about being too busy to eat with me...?'

'I'm too busy to chew, practically. I certainly don't have time to fiddle around with knives and forks.'

He lifted his hands to his face and rubbed his palms over his cheeks. Then he locked his fingers behind his neck and said in a tone of mournful amusement. 'Oh, Lizzy...'

'Now what's that supposed to mean?' she frowned.

'It means that you haven't the first idea of how to run a business.'

'How dare——?'

'Now don't waste energy arguing, Lizzy! Anger can be very draining. Save yourself for all those orders over there...' And he nodded mildly at the pile of mail he'd brought.

She glowered at him, then turned and picked up a lump of clay and began hammering at it with her fists.

'Taking your anger out on that stuff isn't going to help matters.'

She beat the clay more furiously still. 'I'm getting rid of trapped gases, as it happens,' she snapped. 'You have to do this or the pieces explode in the kiln.'

He laughed softly. 'So you aren't going to check your mail, huh?'

'Should I? Is that the first rule of business management or something?'

'I just thought you might be anxious to see if there's a letter from—er—Charlton Hesketh?'

Her skin burned. 'I do *get* personal mail!' she returned challengingly.

'Yes. From a Mrs Anna Stevens. She puts her name and address on the back of the envelope. The last time she wrote she sent some baby photos. They dropped out into your cornflakes, remember?'

She bit hard on the inside of her lip. 'Charlton's away,' she said archly.

'Beyond the reach of the world's postal system, I take it?'

'As it happens, yes.'

'Stockbroking in the remote depths of the Amazon basin, eh?'

'Something like that. Not that it's any of your business.'

'So why didn't you go with him, Lizzy? I can just imagine you paddling his canoe while he bats away the mosquitos with his bowler hat.'

'We don't need to live in each other's pockets,' she muttered coldly.

He paused, letting his grey eyes rove over her. She was wearing a very skimpy white cotton sun-top with her shorts today. Worse luck. She tucked her chin in and looked down. Even her shoulders were blushing, now. Damn!

'How ódd...' he continued drily. 'People do have long-distance relationships like that, of course. But not you, Lizzy. Oh, no. Not you. You're far too intense a creature to make do with love at a distance.'

Her nerve fled. She'd done enough lying already. Anyway, it was pointless. He couldn't have made it more obvious that he'd guessed. But she was not going to be cowed. She met his eye challengingly, and kept staring, her lips pressed tight together.

'In which case,' he added, tilting his head quizzically to one side, and closing the distance between them, 'let's see if I can offer you something a bit closer to home.'

His wrists came to rest lightly on her shoulders. His hands dropped down to lie against her shoulder-blades. The palms were broad, flat, dry against her bare skin. His fingers nudged against her flesh.

Her heart was thundering so hard that she feared her teeth might rattle at any minute. She was coming to dread this roaring sexual need of hers. How long must she go on fighting it? Increasingly she found herself dreaming that she had given in...that she had given herself to

him, body and, inevitably and reluctantly, soul... And
then she would wring as much pain from the image as
possible, forcing herself to imagine him pushing her out
of his bed in the morning so that he could reclaim his
solitude. She had to go on fighting it!

Sex, for Lizzy, was the language of love. If she allowed herself once to make love with him, she knew,
with a deadly certainty, that she would fall hopelessly
and helplessly in love with him. And how ironic that
would be! When she had failed so dismally to find the
right emotions with men who were kind and who liked
her and were ready to love her in return, she was now
having to fight the impulse to give everything to a man
who couldn't have cared less about her as a person. And
yet she didn't draw back from the stimulus of his touch.

'Lizzy?'

'Yes?'

'You're tired.'

'How very perceptive!' Her voice was small and tight.

'Then let me take you to bed. I know the perfect
formula for taking away the aches and pains of the day.'

'I've already had an aspirin, thank you all the same!'

His hands slid around her, so that his arms enclosed
her. She breathed in the raw, male scent of him, while
her skin hissed with pleasure.

'Come to bed with me. We'll have fun. I'll close the
shutters and let the light spill across you in tiger's stripes.'

His arms closed tighter so that she was crushed against
him. His shirt was open. The springy, curling hairs of
his chest brushed against her lips. She had to nip her
tongue between her teeth to prevent herself from licking
wantonly at them.

'No.' The word almost sobbed in her throat, so intense was the urge to say the opposite.

'I don't think Charlton would mind, if that's what's holding you back.' She could hear the laughter behind his voice.

At least, with her face buried against him, he couldn't see the anguished way in which her eyelids briefly screwed closed. '*Don't*...' she muttered furiously '...rub it in!'

He gave a low, delighted growl.

It was that noise; that unmistakable sexual invitation, deep in his throat; that evidence that he wanted nothing from her but the satisfaction of his carnal needs that gave her the courage to fight her way out of the cocooning nest of his arms.

'Leave me alone!' she cried, turning swiftly and running away from her workshop and into the house.

He did leave her alone. Which was to say he didn't touch her again, or refer to Charlton, or invite her to relax with him in his bed in the daytime with the light streaming through the louvred shutters. But he was still there, of course. He still invited her to join him for wine on the terrace, and continued to proffer those devastating, laconic smiles. He still brought out her mail and stood, leaning against the door-frame, watching her work. He spoke to her, briefly, though he still gave nothing away about himself. And when she looked up from her work and met his eye he didn't look away. But the grey eyes which had once been a floorshow of changing responses were now themselves shuttered and barred.

For three whole days she endured this cooler version of Nick, masquerading as the real thing. Then on the third evening she sat down to eat, propped her head on one hand, smiled weakly across the table at Nick, picked up her fork and promptly fell asleep.

She awoke to find herself pillowed in Nick's arms.

'I'm taking you to bed, my girl.' His head was bent close to hers, as it rested woozily against his shoulder. The words stung her consciousness, and her stomach knotted with charged excitement, until she realised that he hadn't meant what she had thought he meant at all. She turned her face into his shoulder to hide her blush. Oh, dear. That was no better. She inhaled his male tang and felt the heat of his skin radiating through his shirt. The innocent physical contact sent warm desire pulsing through her in waves. She kept her face buried in his shirt and feigned sleep for agonising minutes while he carried her upstairs and laid her gently on her bed. When he left her there, softly closing the door behind him, she began to weep. She had wanted him to stay. Tired, unable to think clearly, she was allowing instinct to take over. Because when she applied her mind to the subject she knew perfectly well that if they made love he would end up by breaking her heart.

The next morning he was up with her shortly after dawn. He had never been up that early before, and she was disconcerted by the unfamiliar sense of his presence so early in the day. She hurried out to the workshop as quickly as she could, and started making some new moulds. Within half an hour he was at her side.

'Show me how that's done,' he demanded.

'OK. But why don't you take over while I explain?' she suggested tentatively.

She stood back while he poured the creamy liquid plaster around the finely modelled face.

'Shake it gently,' she instructed. 'So that any air bubbles will rise to the top.'

She watched while he crouched over the mould, agitating it gently but briskly between his strong hands. His long back was stretched even longer as he bowed his head to the task, and the planes of his shoulder-blades stretched taut the cotton of his shirt. His muscular thighs were clearly outlined beneath denim jeans, while his sunbrown forearms were in full view, shadowed by their dark hairs. She couldn't take her eyes off him, and, as usual when she let her gaze rest for too long on his well-made form, the blood started to sing in her veins. Her little inner voice began to whimper wordlessly. Oh, why, oh, why did she want him so much when it was all so unutterably pointless?

'This has gone hard already...' he commented, peering at the damp plaster.

'Mmmm. It goes off very quickly,' she muttered. She should have told him to stop shaking it minutes ago. The mould might well be spoiled. But for once her precious work didn't seem to matter much.

He stood up, stretched hugely then took her by the hand.

She almost jumped out of her skin. 'What are you doing?' she asked fiercely, staring at her palm lying, quiescent, in his large brown hand.

His eyes lit up. 'It's OK,' he said soothingly. 'No one will think we're engaged just because we're holding hands...'

She refused to be amused. 'We're *not* holding hands,' she muttered. '*You're* holding *my* hand. There's a difference.'

He sighed. 'I'm not going to read your palm, Lizzy, if that's what's frightening you. I'm not going to find out the truth about your past, present and future from all those little clay-marked lines. Your secrets are still safe. You don't have to worry.'

He took several paces, pulling her with him. She shuffled reluctantly in his wake.

'Come on,' he said forcefully. 'Unfortunately you don't have a ring through your nose, so I have no option but to lead you by the hand. But I'm only taking you as far as the terrace for breakfast. It's on the table, waiting.'

When they were sitting comfortably he leaned across the table towards her, his chin cupped in his hand.

'Why have you chosen my house for your suicide attempt?' he asked.

'It's not your house.'

'Ah. Then you don't deny it! You *are* trying to kill yourself through over-work.'

'Don't be so stupid. You know why I'm working so hard.'

'I know you don't seem to be looking for a solution to this stupid fix you've got yourself in. And I'm beginning to suspect you of masochistic tendencies since I had to move that revolting van of yours the other day when you boxed me in, after you'd breezed off down to the village to get some more food.

'Cyclops. The one-eyed monster. Whoever was responsible for the design of that dashboard ought to be taken out and shot. Preferably by me. Only a masochist could have paid out good money for a van which puts the evil eye on you every time you get behind the wheel.' He sighed heavily.

She looked away from him. He was sitting there, so calm and relaxed. It was bad enough that he criticised her for working too hard—though considering he'd had to carry her up to bed the previous night perhaps he had some justification. But to criticise her van! That, surely, was her own prerogative!

'It's my business and——'

'And you'll run it yourself. Or let it run you, which is what it looks like from where I'm sitting. But I have no intention of picking up the pieces when it runs you into the ground.'

'I'll advertise for help,' she muttered. To be honest she'd been longing to do just that, but had been afraid that a pair of extra hands around the place would simply mean an extra distraction to Nick.

'Ah. Don't tell me. You'll take out a six-month contract with *Paris Soir* and get two hundred and forty thousand applicants!'

It was no good. She couldn't help laughing. 'No, I shan't. And don't take my laughing at your joke as agreement. I may like your sense of humour, but it doesn't mean you can just butt in and make decisions for me.'

He gave her a wry smile, and then shrugged. 'Finish your breakfast,' he sighed. 'And then go and dig out your swimming things. If the only way I can prevent you from collapsing on me is by taking a day off myself, then it seems that that's what I shall have to do. We're going on a picnic.'

She looked at him in dismay. 'No! I can't possibly let you do that. And anyway, I'm far too busy!'

He said nothing. But he folded his arms and kept on looking at her in a way that let her know that argument was pointless. Eventually, guiltily, she gave him a last pleading look before heading upstairs to put her swimsuit on beneath her shorts and T-shirt.

They went on foot along a small track which wound up the mountainside behind Mon Abri.

'Tell me about this model you made of the house,' he demanded as they got into their stride.

'There's not much to tell,' she began. 'I made it when I was out here for the summer with Grandma. I was just fourteen—a very awkward age. And Grandma was in a funny mood that year. Grandpa had gone off on a bird-watching trip. She was never really right without him. Anyway, it was a very long and boring summer. So I decided to make the model to fill my days.'

He frowned. 'What on earth made you think of doing it? It wasn't exactly an everyday sort of thing for a fourteen-year-old girl to do.'

She smiled wryly. 'Ah, well, I'm afraid I've never managed to run true to type. Actually,' she explained, remembering, 'it all started when I made some little bricks out of earth one day when I was idling around. I looked up at the house and realised that they were a bit like the stones that the buildings round here are made from. So I made hundreds of these little bricks—sort of irregular and stone-shaped, and left them to dry in the sun. Perhaps...' she added wonderingly '...that was where my obsession with clay started. What do you think?'

He shrugged. 'You'd know that better than I. Anyway, did you finish the house?'

'Oh, yes. I even made little tiles. And then I did hundreds of drawings of the furniture and outhouses and everything, so that I could finish it off properly.'

'But you couldn't have done all that in eight weeks?'

'No. Grandma turned up trumps and paid to have it shipped back to England. It was a mammoth great thing, as you can imagine.'

'That's fantastic!' he exclaimed, sounding genuinely enthusiastic. 'So did you make all the furniture?'

'I made quite a lot. And I even made little plants for the garden. We had acres of free time at boarding-school, with nothing much to do,' she explained.

'And do you still have it?'

'No. I'm afraid not. When I got home for the Easter holidays it had—er—gone.'

'Gone?'

'Yes. A misunderstanding,' she said brightly. 'My mother thought I had finished with it.'

'Finished with it? But surely she could see——?'

'And it was an awful nuisance. It took up half my bedroom. Especially since I'd built a plinth at Christmas so I could do the terraced gardens properly.'

'But how on earth——?'

'I was a bit disappointed at the time, of course. But really it was ages ago, and honestly it was neither here nor there. I would soon have got tired of it, anyway.' She stopped talking quickly before the lightness in her voice crumbled.

Nick fell silent, too. So it was a relief when he pointed up ahead, and said, 'We'll stop there...'

Sheltered by a belt of trees was small, ancient stone building. Nick flung himself on to the shaded grass in front of it.

'Time for a rest,' he groaned, though, unlike her, he wasn't breathless at all from the exertion.

She sat beside him, examining the small dwelling. 'Is this somebody's house?' she asked.

He shook his head. 'No. It's for the shepherd's use when he brings the sheep up to these high slopes. It's hardly used these days, though it's still habitable. These sort of buildings are dotted around the mountains—both for the shepherds and for lost travellers. The mountains of the Massif Central may not be the Alps, but they're still pretty treacherous in winter.'

'Is this where we're going to have our picnic? The view is stunning from here.'

'No. There's an even better spot about a mile further on. Just wait till you see it!'

He refused to tell her more, which irritated her. But when they finally arrived she was glad he had said nothing. Words couldn't have done the place justice, and might anyway have spoiled the delicious shock of scrambling down through a small copse to emerge on the banks of a bright, sparkling pool, into which a small waterfall cascaded.

'This is fantastic!' she gasped.

He slapped her on the shoulder. 'Not bad, eh? Our own private picnic spot, complete with swimming-pool.'

It was perfect. The sky above was the light, airy, unspoiled blue of morning, while the water shimmered silver in front of them. They stretched out on the grass, chattering amiably about nothing in particular. Happiness swept in a tidal wave through Lizzy's tired mind. This was heaven. Nick was different today. Less...inaccessible, somehow... As if he had opened a gate in that barrier just a crack.

Though, she thought guiltily, the barriers were still very much there. There was still the business of the house to be sorted out, for a start. She had intended time and again to make an appointment with a lawyer when she went into town. But somehow she was always too frantically busy. Still, she could have written a letter to a lawyer... Though her written French was so laboured, and she had been so very tired... She glanced across at him, wondering whether to bring up the subject now, and apologise for her tardiness. Better not, she decided. It might spoil the wonderful, carefree atmosphere...

Instead she sensed it might be a good moment to question him about his work.

'It must have been exciting, being a foreign correspondent?'

He pulled a sour face. 'At first, yes. But being at the sharp end of human suffering for too long turned out to be soul-destroying. I could see myself becoming a cynical old hack. I seemed to be losing the ability to feel... to care. In the end I faced up to the fact that what I'd always wanted to do was to write stories. The trouble was, the novel I had in mind was about hope, not despair. Stuck endlessly in the world's trouble spots, it was too precious a commodity to squander on a mere story. I had to save what little I had for keeping myself sane.

'Which was why I knew I would have to find a retreat from the clamouring world if ever I was to get that book written. Hence the deal with your grandfather.'

Lizzy turned her head on the springy, dry grass to look at him. His eyes were fixed on the sky. 'And was the book all you wanted? Was it about hope?'

He pulled a face. 'It was about hope, yes. But as to whether it was all I wanted, well, has one of your pots ever satisfied you completely? That's the trouble with creating something from inside. It's never perfect.' He stopped, mulling over his words, then continued, 'And yet... I was happy with the book. It wasn't perfect, of course, but I knew I'd done my best. And it left something still to strive for. It made me want to write the second and the third... Perhaps if I'd achieved perfection then writing would have lost its savour. Maybe all life is like that—an endless desire to build on what you've achieved...to improve...and in the end, perhaps, you look back and decide that in all that struggle lay the very perfection that you thought was so elusive.'

Lizzy threw him an admiring smile. 'You're very wise,' she murmured, and then, embarrassed, added teasingly, 'You don't think you may just have solved the problem of Life, the Universe and Everything there, do you, Nick?'

His response was to tear up a handful of grass and throw it at her before springing to his feet, kicking off his espadrilles and calling 'Race you to the water for a paddle before lunch!'

The water was delectably clear and cold. And the picnic, a simple meal of bread and cheese and salad, washed down with white wine and sparkling mineral water, was as uniquely satisfying as only a meal eaten out of doors could be. Afterwards they lay in the shade and dozed for a while, before Lizzy, opening her eyes to the sight of the clear blue water, suggested a swim.

She knotted her hair on top of her head, then peeled off her shorts and T-shirt, revealing the simple jade one-piece costume beneath. She gave Nick a shy glance, nervous about revealing so much of herself to him, but he was busy pulling his polo shirt over his head. Hastily she ran to the pebbled edge of the water, anxious to avoid having to watch him reveal increasing amounts of his suntanned body. She was equally anxious to avoid seeing his response to her creamy-white skin, peppered across the shoulders with tiny golden freckles. She always felt unattractively pale when bathing. Keeping her back to him she plunged into the water and took a few bold strokes, before finding her feet, and rearing up, gasping for air.

'Cold, isn't it?' Nick laughed, running into the water beside her.

The sight of his broad, muscular frame in brief navy trunks would have brought her out in goose-bumps, had the temperature of the water not beaten him to it.

'It's freezing!' she shrieked, struggling to catch her breath. 'Why didn't you warn me?'

He laughed, scooping up water with a wide sweep of his arm, and splashing her playfully. 'You paddled before lunch,' he accused. 'I thought you knew!'

'The sun must have warmed the shallow water at the edge,' she returned, splashing him back. 'I still think you were mean not to have said.'

But his response was simply to drench her in armfuls of water, which he cast into the air to rain down on her like silver beads.

Playing was the best way to cope with the ice-cold mountain pool, she discovered, and before long they were romping like a couple of children, yelling and shouting as they found new and ingenious ways of drenching the other. After a while Nick led her out into the deeper water to swim across the pool, beyond the waterfall.

'You must . . .' he insisted when she protested. 'It's the best bit, I promise.'

Shuddering at first when she dunked herself, she soon acclimatised to the cold. She followed his powerful crawl with her own accomplished breast-stroke until they reached a small beach beyond the waterfall, half-hidden by over-hanging branches. Nick sprinted out of the water and grabbed hold of a thick piece of knotted rope which hung down amidst the foliage.

'Look,' he explained. 'The local children do this all summer long. They're regular Tarzans around here.' And he clambered up on to a thick branch, grasping the rope in his hands, and then with a powerful thrust of his legs swung out across the water and right through the waterfall. He sent sheaves of water spinning out around him in all directions, before landing on a high ledge of rock beyond. He sent the rope back to her, yelling, 'Your turn now!'

She trembled with fear as she stood on the warm branch, trying to pluck up her courage. It was a long way across, and the ledge looked awfully small. What if she fell off and was forced underwater by the cascading waterfall? But Lizzy's nerves had never failed her yet when it came to a challenge. Taking a deep breath and closing her eyes, she hung on to the rope and leapt. He caught her on the far side, grasping her lightly but firmly at the waist.

She turned unsteadily to him, her eyes shining, her body acutely aware of his gentle hold. 'That was brilliant!' she exclaimed, in a voice which shook slightly from the confusing mixture of emotions.

He looked down on her face, his eyes dark and bewilderingly intense. Then without warning he lifted his hands from her waist, turned sharply away, and arced his body into an impressive dive, which carried him swiftly and elegantly into the air, before sweeping him down cleanly into the sparkling water below.

He had disappeared from the rock beside her so abruptly. She had seen him only in motion. And the moment was so brief that she could easily have been mistaken. Except that she knew that she wasn't. He had made the dive to hide from her the signs of his arousal, hard beneath the dark, clinging fabric of his swimming trunks. Shocked, she grabbed the rope to swing herself back to the safety of the little beach, scarcely registering when she sliced through the wall of water to land securely on the far side.

He had already swum back to shore, and was striding back to sit on the grass from where he gave her a careless wave. She raised her own hand in response, hoping that she was giving an impression of carefree *joie de vivre*. Inside she was struggling to quell her turmoil.

Despite his earlier attempts to persuade her into his bed, sex had not exactly been on offer for some days now. She had assumed that once he had realised that her body wasn't part of the special introductory package he had scrubbed the idea, probably as grateful to skirt complications of that sort as she had tried to be.

All he *really* wanted was that she go away as suddenly as she had arrived. But now she found herself praying that this was a sign that she was more than just a conveniently handy female, who might have served a purpose had she been willing. She had no illusions about his response to her as a person. She was an irritation. No more. But could it be that he genuinely desired her? She sighed. She mustn't start fooling herself. It had just been an unwelcome, fleeting response. Which was why he had dived off the ledge so quickly, before something happened which he might regret. And just as well, she scolded herself, ashamed to find herself hoping otherwise . . .

She looked warily down at her own outline. Slim, with a narrow waist, the length of her legs accentuated by the cut of the swimsuit, she supposed she must look—if not exactly alluring—then at least unmistakably *female* in the body-hugging swimwear. She allowed her eyes to assess her breasts. They were full, firm and high, and the glossy jade-green fabric outlined them perfectly, even hinting at the pink aureole around the nipples. Oh, no! She really ought to have known better from the moment he mentioned swimming. Still, she comforted herself, at least he'd put himself quickly out of temptation's way. It must just have been an automatic reaction to the sight of her swirling through the waterfall, haloed by spray. After all, he'd looked quite spectacular doing the same thing. Determined to behave as if she had noticed nothing, she swam back to join him.

She kept up a cheery stream of chatter as she sat beside him on the grass, hugging her knees to her chest, and munching on a crisp apple. She wanted more than any-thing to change out of her wet costume. But they had brought no towels. She had nothing to hide under while she changed, and if she simply popped her T-shirt on over her swimsuit, it would soon be just as wet and just as revealing, and, being cotton, would take a lot longer to dry. There was nothing for it but to sit it out. The fabric would soon dry in this heat, even though they were in the shade of a tree.

He was stretched out on his stomach, his head turned towards her. 'You're beginning to burn, Lizzy,' he ob-served, interrupting her flow of chatter.

'Oh, no! The water will have washed off my sun-block cream,' she groaned. 'We were in the water for ages, and I was standing up most of the time in the full sun.' Now that it had been mentioned she had become aware of the mild burning sensation on her shoulders and the back of her neck. She rummaged in her bag for the cream.

He had pulled himself on to his knees, and before she could protest he had taken it out of her hands and was unscrewing the cap. 'I'll do your shoulders and the back of your neck first,' he remarked, squeezing a large blob out on to his hands. 'That's where the sun has caught you worst—probably because the skin there's usually covered by your hair and hasn't had a chance to get acclimatised.'

She gulped. The last thing she wanted was for him to start rubbing the cream into her back. And yet if she snatched it from him and began tortuously trying to get it on to her own shoulder-blades, she'd end up practically thrusting her breasts under his nose. There was no way of rubbing her own back while preserving her modesty.

He started to massage the cool cream into her nape. The sensation of his hands moving across her back with smooth, even strokes had an instantaneously arousing effect on her. She was used to the daily prickle of awareness: the tightness of her skin whenever she was with him; the soft, suffusing heat that surged from a place deep inside to warm every last inch of her. And she remembered each moment of that kiss, when she had tasted a rush of molten desire so strong that it had taken her breath away. But this was everything the kiss had been . . . and yet far more potent still.

As his fingers plied her skin, her breasts seemed to swell against the crush of her knees. Her nipples, which had tightened against the cold water, were now proudly and throbbingly erect. Her lips had parted slightly, and to her astonishment she could hear her own breath surging unevenly. She was almost gasping with desire!

His hands had come up to grasp her shoulders. For a moment the grip was firm, and then suddenly his hands relaxed and dropped over her shoulders to rest lightly on her hunched knees. For a brief moment the hairs of his chest brushed delicately against her back. Then before she could understand what was happening his face was in her hair and he was nibbling gently at the nape of her neck with his firm lips. He pulled her round to face him, and with a low groan of desire he began to kiss her. She was shaking beneath the firm hold of his hands—shaking not with fear but with the inescapable yearning which held her mesmerised.

She began to return his kiss rapturously, her own hands twining in his hair, while his explored the contours of her back. Before she knew it they were stretched out together on the dappled grass, his heavy, muscular thigh resting across hers, his mouth exploring her own, while she wantonly ran her fingers over his shoulders and across the hard planes of his chest. For what seemed like an eternity their mouths expressed a world beyond words. Then his hand came round to cup her breast. For a moment he was still, seeming to relish the fullness of it in his palm. At last his thumb gravely traced the contours of her nipple, encircling it time and again with a teasing lightness.

She pulled her mouth away from his, scarcely able to breathe as sharp daggers of pleasure darted from her breasts to that dark, velvet place within, which was throbbing out its excited response. Small sounds of pleasure escaped from her throat as his fingers eased the damp fabric away from her breast, letting it spill out into his hand. Then the rosy pink nipple felt the rough sweep of his chin as his lips enclosed it, drawing her deep into his caressing mouth.

Her arousal moved on to another plane as her breasts throbbed against the gentle nip of his teeth. Now there was something urgent...demanding...pulsing hard inside her—pleading for its delectable release. This exquisite, questing, sharp beat of her desire brought her body inching closer to his, moving instinctively to crush against the swell of his hard arousal.

It was the burning need of her own body which jarred her mind into awareness at last. She wanted him so badly. She wanted him inside her. She wanted that carnal ache satisfied by the hard maleness of him. Shocked by the force of her own instinct, she dragged herself free of his arms, and rolled over on the grass to lie apart from him, her face buried in her hands. She struggled to still her ragged breathing and to hush the small moans which escaped her lips.

'I'm sorry,' she whispered. 'I'm sorry, Nick—but I mustn't...' And then suddenly, burningly, she wanted more than anything in the world to be back in his arms. Oh, why had she been so impulsive? He had only to say the word...

He had come to sit close to her, one large hand stroking her hair reassuringly. She heard him strive to master his own breathing, but his voice when it came was clotted with desire. 'Oh, Lizzy...' His breath hissed between his teeth. 'Why not? Why not...?' he groaned, almost painfully.

'No...' The word came out in a strangled whisper. 'I'm sorry.'

And yet what had she wanted him to say? That he cared? She wasn't that much of a fool! No. She had wanted some indication...some hint...that he wanted *her*—her especially. Not just because she was a woman. Not just because she was there...

She didn't really know which words would have wrought that magic... And yet still she ached for the sign that would free her to scurry back into the sweet cradle of his embrace.

He blew out his breath in a sharp burst. 'For God's sake don't apologise!' he commanded harshly. 'I don't force women to make love with me!'

'But I *am* sorry,' she insisted, peeping gratefully between her fingers to meet his eye. But he turned his head away.

There was a long pause. Nick's eyes had narrowed and he was looking out over the water. He swallowed hard then said in a voice that was once more controlled and easy, 'Do you want to tell me what it's all about?'

'I...I just don't want to make love with you,' she murmured helplessly.

'Well, that's not true, and we both damn well know it!' he responded condemningly.

She could hardly contradict him after her body had betrayed her so flagrantly. And yet she was lost for words. There was no way that she could explain.

'I may find you attractive, but I...don't...want to make love with you, Nick. I just don't,' she floundered, tugging on her clothes.

'It's something you want to happen inside marriage? Is that what you mean?' he suggested.

She was silent. She could hardly tell him what sex would mean for her. How impossible it would be for her to hold back that fountain of emotion... How she would want his love in return... Good grief! All *Nick* wanted was his solitude back...

He frowned, looking down at his own hands. 'There hasn't been... someone... a bad experience?' he asked gruffly.

She shook her head. 'No,' she responded weakly. 'Nothing like that. Honestly.'

'Then why not?'

Why not? So he still thought that a casual sexual affair was a natural outcome of sharing the same roof, after all. She stood up and wandered to the water's edge, keeping her back to him.

'I'll tell you why not,' she said sourly at last. 'Because I don't want you. Not under any circumstances. There's nothing to explain. Nothing for you to go nosing out. No secrets. Just the plain fact that I don't want you. All I want is my work... And my house,' she added as a bitter afterthought.

She stopped talking quickly, before something in her voice cracked and gave her away. Nick too, was strangely silent. He gathered together the picnic things, and began to walk away. She struggled to keep pace with him. Oh, damn it! Damn it all to hell!

It had been a perfect day. But now it was all spoiled. She walked along beside him in silence. She was feeling far too choked even to try to get any conversation going, and now Nick had clammed up too.

CHAPTER FIVE

NICK didn't eat at Mon Abri that evening. When they arrived back—the uncomfortable silence chafing like a wound between them—he went into the kitchen and made her a coffee as if to indicate that things really were much the same as before. But of course they weren't, and no amount of hot drinks could convince her otherwise. He took his coffee upstairs with him to work. But his typewriter was uncommonly silent.

Lizzy sat in the comfortable living-room for a while, sipping her drink, and trying to quash the bitter memories of the afternoon. It had been so wonderful. And now it was all spoiled, just because she hadn't had the sense to keep to her work.

Her work, after all, was the most important thing in her life. Letting herself get all wound up about a man whose interest in her was non-existent was the most stupid thing she'd ever done in her life. If he'd shown signs of *liking* her it might be different. If he'd just wanted her around... needed her company... found her attractive in her own right, instead of simply a convenient means of satisfying his carnal desires... She sighed so heavily that it felt as if the last drop of breath was juddering out of her body.

Then she propped her elbow on her knee, cupped her chin in her hand and—thus hunched mournfully on the voluptuous cream sofa—gave herself a good talking to. It didn't help much. But at least she felt she'd tried.

Lizzy had grown very used to looking on the bright side of all sorts of things, over the years.

At last she did find a way of consoling herself that it had all been for the best. He was a full-blooded male of the species. He couldn't have that many opportunities, closeted away here on the borders of a conventional little French village, to fulfil his sexual needs. So she could hardly blame him for trying, especially as she'd come and plonked herself down in his house, and fixed her eyes longingly on his forearms. Nor could she blame him for wanting nothing more from her than that. He'd chosen his solitary way of life, after all, and at least he hadn't made a pretence of liking her in order to seduce her. No, he was a sensible, self-contained man, who lived for his work. And she was a sensible and self-contained woman who lived for hers. The world hadn't come crashing down when she'd repelled· his advances in the past. And nor would it this time.

He would be blaming her, of course, which was why he had been so quiet on the way back. But he'd made the effort to seem understanding, even though she could sense he was having to keep some fairly thunderous feelings in check. So surely things would be back to normal by the morning?

But when he came downstairs at about seven it was to tell her that he wouldn't be there in the morning.

'I'm going to Montpellier for a few days,' he explained.

She took in his altered appearance—the freshly shaven jaw without its usual blue bloom—the cream linen suit— the immaculate trouser-creases. He was even wearing a tie, and had discreetly dropped a briefcase and overnight bag at the foot of the stairs.

'I see,' she nodded with a tight little smile.

He came to sit on the sofa opposite her, hitching the cloth of his well-cut trousers in a way that he never had to do when he was wearing jeans or shorts. It made it seem as if he had changed more than just his clothes. He leaned forwards, resting his forearms on his thighs as he spoke. 'I have various things to attend to there. I shall only be gone for two or three days at the most. Madame Roget will cook for you, of course, so you don't need to worry——'

Her quick temper flashed smartly. 'I'm quite capable of looking after myself! I've been doing it since I was eight, after all!'

'Eight?' He gave her a disbelieving frown.

'Yes. Oh, I didn't cook my own meals at eight, but that was the age at which I first went to boarding-school. You learn to be independent very quickly in that sort of set-up, you know? So you don't have to assume that just because I'm a bit scatterbrained sometimes I'm not capable of fending for myself perfectly well.'

He gave her a sour smile. 'I would *never* assume that of you, Lizzy,' he said drily. 'As it happens, I was thinking of Madame Roget . . . I shouldn't want her to feel useless . . .'

'Oh. Well. In that case——'

'Anyway,' he cut in, his face suddenly becoming grave, 'I thought I'd better let you know why I'm going.'

'You really don't need to,' she sparked defensively. 'Good gracious, you're a free agent! You can do exactly as you please. What you choose to do with your time is entirely your affair.'

Something glittered, hard and cold in his eyes. 'And just what is that supposed to mean? If you're referring to this afternoon's escapade, then perhaps I should remind you that it takes two...'

She bit her lip as hard as she dared without actually drawing blood. 'I didn't mean that at all, as it happens,' she said wearily. 'Honestly, I know it was my fault——'

'Lizzy,' he said roughly, 'let's not talk about faults. What's done is done. We both wanted it...at least at the start. And you had every right to call a halt whenever you liked. Now if you don't mind I'd rather drop the subject.' He glared at her.

She had to give him credit for saying the right thing, even if he wasn't feeling it. She proffered a stiff smile.

'Now, to go back to what I was trying to say earlier. I'm going to Montpellier to see my lawyer. I think it's about time we began to get this business of the house sorted out. It will be better for both our sakes.'

She nodded in what she hoped was a reasonable and sage manner. He had every right to see a solicitor. Why, he should have done it weeks ago when she'd first arrived! It was something she'd been meaning to do herself. There was no reason in the world why she should feel hurt by it. None at all. 'Good plan,' she murmured, forcing her lips to form the words.

Fleetingly she found herself wondering why he hadn't made a start on sorting out this mess before now. Presumably he'd gone on expecting that they could get some sort of sexual relationship off the ground if only he could keep the open hostilities to a minimum. Well, now he knew different. It was what she'd wanted, so she really ought to be delighted. Considering how fervently she'd hoped to avoid falling into his bed, this clear-cut sign that he no longer had any desire to tempt her there ought

to have had her dancing for joy. But molten lead seemed
to have accumulated in her veins. As for dancing, she
doubted she could even move...

'I'm glad you understand.' He was getting to his feet,
an unnaturally formal smile gracing his features. 'I'm
driving down this evening so that I can make an early
start.' And he strode across the room, looking every inch
the businessman in his suit. Then he picked up his
gleaming black leather bags and left.

She kept the fatuous smile on her face until she heard
the engine of the Range Rover roar into life. And then
she burst into tears.

She slept fitfully. The next morning she awoke feeling
grey and tired. So much for having a day off! Nick had
hardly ever been around when she got up and started
working, but she missed him even so. It began to dawn
on her that for the past days her existence had been
lightened by the mere possibility of his appearing in the
workshop, his lazy eyes resting on her while she worked.
And as for those mealtimes, when they would sit together
on the terrace, sipping wine, exchanging comments...

She found herself working painfully slowly. Madame
Roget laid her lunch out on the pine table before leaving,
but it was not the same, eating alone. She carried her
plate up to her room, dragging out each step to use up
a little more of that infernal time. As she passed Nick's
bedroom she couldn't resist opening the door and
peeping in. It was scrupulously tidy and surprisingly
bare. There was no watch, no pile of loose change on
the chest of drawers. No photos in frames beside the
huge bed. She was disappointed. But why? She had been
alone in the house many times, but she'd never been

tempted to sneak a look at his bedroom before. What
was it she was looking for now?

Behind the scent of polish Lizzy could smell the indefinable maleness of him. She hurriedly retreated to
the landing. The next door led to Nick's study. She had
never been in there either, though she had glimpsed the
clutter of books and papers through the open door on
several occasions.

She went in, and sat at his desk. It faced the french
window which opened on to the veranda. The typewriter
had an empty piece of paper rolled into it. To the side
of the desk was a mesh tray, stacked high with closely
typed paper. She picked up the top sheet and glanced at
it. 'Chapter One...' she read. It was Nick's latest manuscript. Idly nibbling at a piece of cucumber, she let her
eyes scan the written word.

When she next looked at her watch a full hour had
passed. She really ought to be getting back to work—
but first she must just find out what happened next...

Her lunch break dragged on for another twenty-five
minutes before she managed to wrench herself away from
the unfolding story and hurry back down to the
workshop. The novel was extraordinarily good. As good
as anything she had ever read—and Lizzy was a vo-
racious reader. She couldn't wait to down tools at seven
and return to the book.

She read, stopping only to bolt down Madame Roget's
delicious casserole at nine, until she reached the last page.
The story, of course wasn't finished. It was maddening!
It was so very absorbing...and there was no way of
guessing what the end would be.

Quite early on in her reading, it had dawned on Lizzy
that she had already read Nick's two earlier books—with

equal enjoyment—though she hadn't made the con-
nection before, as he wrote under a pseudonym. This
latest manuscript formed the final part of a trilogy—or
perhaps only the third of a quartet. There was no way
of telling.

The books followed the fortunes of a woman and her
family, from her colonial childhood in the West Indies
early in the century through to the present day. When
the woman married she was brought to her husband's
house in the mountains of France. As Lizzy turned the
pages it became compellingly clear to her that the setting
was Mon Abri itself. The descriptions were so tellingly
evocative. But Mon Abri was more than just a backdrop
against which the characters lived out their lives. The
house itself, in all three books, came to symbolise stab-
ility, family loyalty, permanence—even love itself. What
was it Nick had said? He had wanted to write about
hope, not despair? He had certainly succeeded ... And
this house was at the very core of his success.

Sitting at Nick's desk, looking out into the dark of
night, Lizzy knew that she could never claim Mon Abri
from Nick now. His home was his inspiration. It was
not just a roof over his head, but the source of his muse.
The very fabric of the walls was written into his work.
Even the garden was woven into the plot. The terraced
beds were planted with pinks and anemones, irises and
narcissi, roses and lilacs and lily of the valley. Through
Nick's writing she saw a young husband planting the
flowers to woo his English-born wife. And from the
tender shoots of a fragile marriage grew a sturdy, per-
ennial love. Tears started to Lizzy's eyes. The books had
been nurtured in this house. Their roots were here with
Nick. She still didn't understand the man who wrote them

any better. But at least she understood how important the house was in his life.

She wandered desolately back to her bedroom and stared hard at her reflection in the mirror. She knew what she had to do, now. She would stay only for as long as her business required—assuming Nick would let her.

He was annoyed with her. Their friendship was marred by the sexual pull he exerted on her. And now he had gone to find a lawyer to prove that Mon Abri was his. He clearly couldn't bear to have her there any longer. When he came back she would tell him that he needn't bother with the law. He could have the house. Quite soon she should have enough money to rent somewhere else to live and work.

It ought to have hurt, the idea of leaving Mon Abri. When she had arrived just a couple of weeks before, she had felt that she was coming home at last. But, ironically, without Nick's presence to bring life to it, the house suddenly felt alien and cold. It would be better to leave.

He had said two or maybe three days. When forty-seven hours had passed she started to strain for the sound of an engine labouring up the winding track. But all she heard were leaves rattling drily in the warm air. It was the same all evening, her ears perpetually tuned in for the sound of the Range Rover. Twice she woke in the night, convinced that she had heard something, but when she peeped out of the window to the yard in front of the garage there was only the faint shape of the van looming out of the darkness.

He arrived back in the middle of the afternoon. She was pouring a mould at the time, luckily, so she couldn't obey the impulse to run out and greet him. But her ears registered the decisive slamming of the car door, and the firm crunch of his footfalls on the gravel. He had gone straight to the house without coming to see her first.

Having finished the mould, she tried hard to find little jobs to occupy her for a while. She didn't want him to think she was impatient to see him, though she couldn't hide her own anxiety from herself.

In the event it was he who came to find her—though not for nearly an hour.

'Lizzy?' He was dressed once again in well-fitting jeans and a polo shirt. And there was a faint hint of stubble on his chin. He looked himself again. But, she tried reminding herself sternly, he was still the inaccessible stranger who had walked out of the door three days earlier.

'Hi,' she sighed, sucking at the insides of her cheeks to prevent a huge, involuntary grin from plastering itself all over her face. She had a suspicion that her eyes were doing as much smiling as was necessary, anyway.

He had a glass of wine in each hand. 'Have I interrupted you at a crucial moment, or can you spare a few minutes to come and drink this?'

Things really were back to normal! 'I'll just wash my hands,' she gasped eagerly, rushing to the sink in the corner to scrub away the day's grime.

He was waiting for her out on the terrace, nursing his glass in his hands.

'How did things go?' she asked in what she hoped was a neutral voice.

He grimaced. 'I've uncovered a bit of a hornet's next, I'm afraid.' He sighed. Then he stretched back in his chair, easing out the muscles of his shoulders, and dropping his head back to study the sky.

'What did the *notaire* say?' she asked. Now that she had made up her mind to let him have the house the question was a lot easier than it might have been.

He pulled a sour face. 'It's very complicated. Actually, I'd rather talk about all that later, if you don't mind. What about coming into Albi with me tonight for a meal? I know of a stunning little restaurant where the food's out of this world.'

Her brows arched with pleasure. Apart from the picnic they'd never spent time together anywhere but at this house. Though he'd often casually suggested that she stroll down to the village with him and spend an hour sitting outside the café with a glass of the local wine or a *café au lait*. But she'd always protested that she'd been too busy. Going all the way to Albi to a restaurant was a different kettle of fish altogether. Especially now that she'd made up her mind to leave. She wanted to grab as much time with him as she possibly could.

'OK,' she conceded, as if it were neither here nor there. 'It sounds nice.' Then she flashed him a maverick grin. 'So it's bad news for me, huh? He's said that you've got by far the best claim? You want to break the news to me somewhere where I can't smash a bottle over your head?'

'*She* said nothing of the sort,' he responded wryly. 'I'd just rather not talk about it till later. OK?'

'OK,' she echoed, visualising Nick discussing her with a sleek French beauty, silky-haired and long-legged, wearing sheer stockings and a beautifully tailored suit. Jealousy snipped at her equilibrium with razor-sharp blades.

'What shall we talk about, in that case?' she asked, forcing her inner eye to shut out the offending image.

He shrugged. 'I don't know. I'm tired. Entertain me. Tell me more about yourself.'

'I'm glad you think I'm a source of amusement,' she commented sarcastically, though she was secretly pleased at the relaxed way in which he was treating her.

'Go on . . .' he cajoled. 'Tell me about this boarding-school of yours . . .'

'I'm afraid there's nothing much to tell. It was a girls' preparatory and grammar school in Kent. It had all the trappings of a rather starchy place. You know—uniforms and hockey sticks and Matron in the sanatorium. But actually it wasn't particularly strict at all. Probably because there were lots of day girls there. Most of the boarders were over eleven, so for the first few years we younger boarders were quite coddled by the housemistresses. I liked it.'

'Why did you go? Was your father in the army or working abroad?'

She shook her head. It was a question she was rather uncomfortable answering, but she'd had lots of practice. Hopefully it would come out all pat, and she wouldn't end up sounding pathetic. 'No. That was the usual reason for younger girls having to board, of course. But in my case it was because my parents wanted to treat me and my brother fairly. He went to prep school at eight, so I did too.'

There! She'd managed it without giving away the fact that her parents had moved house so that her brother could be a day pupil at the school of their choice!

Nick straightened in his chair and opened his eyes. His face wore a curious expression. Brittle. Hard, almost. He drained his glass, slamming it on the table just an iota too hard.

'So what did you do while I was away?' he asked at length. She sent up a grateful prayer. Thank goodness he'd stopped talking about her childhood!

'Worked,' she said simply. Then she gave him an awkward smile. 'And I'm afraid I did something rather cheeky...' She stopped herself. For some reason she couldn't quite bring herself to confess to having read his book. Of course, she shouldn't have gone into his room like that. And she certainly shouldn't have read his unfinished manuscript. She'd asked him several times to look out his two published works for her to read, but he'd always responded rather vaguely and hadn't followed it up. Even so, it wasn't fear of his wrath that held her back. It was more that she didn't want him to know that she realised how important the house was to his work. It was too intimate... too personal somehow. Presumably that was why he had always been so very evasive about his work. He felt it too. A little prickle of happiness started inside her. At last she was beginning to get a little glimpse—however slight—of the man himself.

'Have you gone to sleep?'

'Pardon?'

'You tailed off in mid-sentence. You were going to tell me about this other thing you did?'

'Was I?' She frowned. 'Oh, yes. I—er—cooked a meal.'

'I see. A cheeky meal?'

'Well, no. Not exactly. But I...borrowed some of your spices.' She smiled in what she hoped was a cheeky fashion. 'Without asking,' she added, to emphasise the point.

He ran his thumb along the line of his jaw, watching her languidly. 'And you sent a portion off in the post to Charlton, I take it!'

She looked at him suspiciously. 'And just what is that supposed to mean?'

'It means you're not telling me the truth, Lizzy. That's all.' He pushed his glass across the table and got to his feet. He took his time. There was nothing to suggest annoyance in his stance. But his eyes told a different story.

Lizzy's skin was stained with guilt. She looked enviously at his sun-bronzed face. Camouflage! Who on earth would choose to be born a redhead?

'I don't have to tell you everything!' she muttered defensively.

He shrugged. 'Lizzy,' he drawled, 'you don't have to tell me *anything*.' And before she could reply he had walked away.

She allowed herself plenty of time to get ready. She spent ages in the shower trying to shampoo away her sense of embarrassment. She *hated* lying. She'd never done it before. So why did she keep on finding herself in situations with him where the truth just wouldn't seem to do? It was his fault. It really was. She wasn't going to waste time trying to get a fair-minded perspective on it. Why should she? If he would just *react* to her like a normal human being then she could behave normally, too. She stuck her head under the jet of water and let it run into her eyes. Yowch! That was better. She reached blindly for a towel. You couldn't think much when your eyes were full of soap!

It hadn't really been such a good idea. Putting mascara on, for instance, when your eyes were puffy and bloodshot was not easy. She managed it at the third attempt. Damn. Now she looked as if she had been crying. And that was the last thing she wanted.

In the end she ran out of time long before she was dressed. He rapped impatiently on her bedroom door.

'Dinner, I said, Lizzy. Not breakfast!'

'I won't be a minute...'

She frantically ran her eyes over her collection of dresses. They were mostly nineteen-thirties originals. She bought them because she loved the quality of workmanship—the fine pin-tucks and panels and buttons. And she liked the clinging, drapey fabrics, and the antique-stall prices. But most of all she liked the way the styles of that era flattered her tiny waist and her rounded breasts. Or, at least, that was what she'd used to like about them. She seriously considered reverting to shorts and a T-shirt before finally settling on a modest pale blue silk crêpe, with a sweetheart neckline, and a bloused bodice which nipped in at the waist before flaring out into a beautifully cut gored skirt.

'Lizzy. For God's sake...'

'It's all right. Don't worry. I'm coming...'

She slipped her feet into a pair of sandals, tore the towel off her hair and ran her fingers hurriedly through the wet curls. Hairdriers always turned her hair into a fuzzy mess, anyway. Never mind. It would be practically dry by the time they got there.

He didn't comment on her appearance. To her immense irritation he hadn't dressed up at all. Unless you counted a fresh polo shirt with his jeans, and a thin blue cotton jacket hooked carelessly over his shoulder by one finger.

He drove expertly on the deserted road, handling the bends with a precision she envied. He didn't say a word. She kept glancing at his profile, but the outline of his long, blunt nose and the curve of his chin didn't reveal much about his state of mind.

At last she could bear the silence no longer.

'Are you in a bad mood?'

'No. But you are.'

'I'm not.'

'Good.'

Silence, she decided, had its good points after all.

When they arrived she clambered down from the Range Rover and stood waiting for him to lock the door. She felt terribly self-conscious, all dressed up while he was looking so casual. She held her chin at a defiant angle. There was nothing wrong in looking good...

And she couldn't help being pleased when he came around to her side of the vehicle, and stopped to survey her with a distinctly appreciative light in his eyes.

'You look absolutely gorgeous...' he growled.

She was quite taken aback. After that second evening when he'd tried to lead up to the kiss by claiming he liked her hair, he'd never once commented on her appearance. This time his voice was husky with some emotion Lizzy couldn't identify. It couldn't be that he was starting to appreciate her for herself, could it?

'Thank you,' she murmured, her chin raising itself fractionally higher. She lifted a hand and tentatively ran her fingers through her curls. They were barely damp. Excellent.

'In fact,' he continued, running his eyes up and down her yet again, 'you look fantastic. But I don't think you'd better go in the restaurant looking like that.'

She frowned at him, her eyes startled.

'Your dress, Lizzy, is soaking wet. It's bordering on the obscene...'

She looked down in horrified dismay. Her hair, clamped between her back and the car seat, had released its moisture into the fine crêpe. Now the discreetly bloused bodice clung to her like a second skin. 'Oh, lord...' she groaned wearily.

He laughed. First his eyes crinkled attractively at the corners, and then he threw back his head and laughed. He'd laughed like that on the first day...

'I thought it had suddenly got a bit cold...' she said bleakly, folding her arms to preserve her modesty. And then his infectious laughter began to penetrate her consciousness. Her shoulders started to shake, and before she knew it she was giggling helplessly with him.

He held out his cotton jacket for her. She shrugged it on and began rolling back the sleeves.

'Come on,' he said, grasping her by the shoulder. 'I'm starved.'

The restaurant was small and informal. Despite the simple décor, the food surpassed anything that Lizzy had ever before tasted. In London cuisine of this sort would have commanded top prices—and attracted a clientele to match. But here in Albi it was served by the chef's wife to anyone in the locality who appreciated good food. The prices would have deterred no one.

Nick was full of teasing good humour throughout the meal, but refused to be drawn on the outcome of his meeting with the lawyer.

'I think it's horrible of you to keep me in suspense like this,' Lizzy frowned, taking a mouthful of veal cooked in white wine. 'Just tell me one little thing that she said?'

Nick nibbled at the corner of his mouth, trying not to laugh. 'OK,' he conceded. 'She told me not to discuss any of this with you. She reminded me that you were an adversary in law, and that it would be unwise to reveal my hand.'

Lizzy screwed up her nose. 'And you'll do just as she says, like a good little boy, huh?' she challenged.

He simply smiled enigmatically and turned back to his meal. It wasn't until she had licked clean the spoon with which she had scooped up her *tarte aux fraises* that Nick consented to talk about his visit to Montpellier.

'Look, Lizzy,' he began gravely, 'the first thing I should say is that things are worse than I ever expected. We aren't talking about one simple court case, but a whole series, one dependent on the outcome of the other. In other words, it will take years to unravel the ownership question. And it will cost maybe two or three times the value of the house in legal fees. You ought to see a lawyer yourself. You really must explain your case to someone who's looking out for *your* interests.'

She avoided meeting his eyes. 'Thanks,' she said quietly. 'I appreciate your saying that. Really. But I think I ought to tell you that I won't be pressing my claim through the legal channels.'

He eyed her warily. 'But why? After all, you were the one who said we should get the lawyers to sort it out. It really is a very complex business. You *will* need good advice.'

She shook her head. 'No. You see, I think it would be best if I let you hang on to Mon Abri. After all, you paid Grandpa for it. It hasn't cost me a penny.'

He leaned back in his chair, sipping his wine. His eyes narrowed as they surveyed her thoughtfully. 'But what about your pots?' he asked at length.

She shrugged apologetically. 'Well, the business has taken off so spectacularly well that I can afford to rent somewhere. It's not the big problem that it was when I first arrived. It shouldn't take me more than a couple of weeks to find a place.'

The last thing she wanted was to reveal to him how truly moved she had been by his writing. Even if she could have brought herself to spell it out, she couldn't bear the idea that he might feel that he ought to be grateful to her. She just wanted him to accept it as a perfectly rational decision.

'And your grandmother's wishes? Don't they count for anything any more?'

She examined her nails for non-existent traces of clay. She was going to have to lie again...

'Not much. Grandma wasn't the sort of person that you could get sentimental about. And anyway, Grandpa sold *you* the house. I loved him too.' She took a deep breath. 'When I came, the idea was to get my business started somewhere where the overheads would be low. Well, I don't need to worry about that quite so much now!'

When she dared look up she was expecting him to look at least mildly pleased. Instead of which his face was unusually pale, his features hard and indecipherable.

'And if I agree to this extraordinary decision of yours, how will I know that you won't change your mind in a month or two when you run out of cash?'

'I wouldn't.' She looked steadfastly at him.

'Lizzy. You sold up everything you had and came running out here on a whim. And yet you're asking me to believe——'

'I'll—er...' Oh, dear. She couldn't deny being rather impulsive at times. But nor could she explain the truth. 'I'll sign a document, waiving my claim.'

'You might just as well waive your claim to the throne of England. If you don't go to court to prove that you've got a claim in the first place, signing away your rights is going to be pretty meaningless from a legal point of view.'

'But I'm not *going* to run out of cash...' she protested. 'I'm up to my eyes in orders. You know that!'

He waited for a long time before he spoke. And when he did Lizzy could hardly believe her ears.

'So it's money after all!' he sneered. 'Money that drives you, just like everyone else!'

'That doesn't make sense...' she cried, wounded by the unfairness of his accusation.

'Doesn't it?' he ventured. 'Are you sure that you haven't seen a *notaire* on one of your little trips into town?'

'No!' she exclaimed heatedly. 'I would have told you if I had! Surely you know me better than that?'

He let his eyes run over her scathingly. It almost *hurt* to be looked at like that by him. He shrugged. 'I was advised not to discuss any of this with you. It would be odd if your lawyer hadn't told you the same thing.'

'But I wouldn't lie! If I *had* been told that, and if I'd decided to act on it, I would at least have told you as much.'

'Would you?' His voice was frozen, laced with disbelief. 'Was *that* the rather cheeky thing you did while I was away? Went to see a lawyer of your own? I'm not terribly impressed by your claims of being so transparently honest, Lizzy. You've been arming yourself for a fight, while I've been gone, haven't you?'

If they hadn't been in a restaurant Lizzy would surely have thrown something at him by now. As it was she sat unnaturally still, pressing her lips hard together and desperately trying to hang on to the remnants of her temper.

'So you didn't already know about this legal quagmire? You didn't know about the years of trailing back and forth to lawyers and courts? And you certainly didn't know about the expense, did you?' He made an explosive noise of disbelief.

'I still don't understand...' she muttered furiously. Surely all these difficulties should have made him even more pleased that she was giving up her claim on the house, not less?

His face still wore the marks of disdain. 'So you claim not to understand? But I think I do.' Again he paused to let his eyes scour her. 'Impatient, impetuous Lizzy,' he continued sarcastically. 'You certainly couldn't wait for the due process of law to deliver its uncertain verdict, could you? Especially when you stood to lose every penny of the fat profit you're making from your business.'

This was too much! She couldn't believe what she was hearing. Her face aflame, she stumbled to her feet, drew herself up to her full five feet five inches, threw back her head and swept out of the restaurant. From her dignified posture he couldn't possibly have guessed how weak her legs felt beneath her. Nor how light-headed she was from the white-hot rage which boiled inside. What on earth had happened to him? How could he possibly think so badly of her? The thought sent an icy shiver running through her. She couldn't bear the idea that he believed she was manipulating him for her own gain . . .

She was no sooner out in the cool evening air than his long strides brought him to her side.

'Go away!' she raged, her voice unsteady.

'You're the one that's going away. Not me . . .' he said with bitter sarcasm.

She began to run. He strode out more purposefully, keeping pace with her with ease.

'It's dark, Lizzy. You're wearing a wet dress and you've nowhere to run!'

He was right. Only once in her life had she found somewhere in the world to run. Mon Abri. 'My Shelter'. And she had fled there as fast as that awful van would carry her. She stopped abruptly. Her face was white and set.

'Is that what you think?' her voice stopped shaking and took on a fierce strength. 'That I've nowhere to go?' She let out a bitter laugh. 'Why do you think I come into Albi so often, Nick? His name may not be Charlton, but . . .' Her voice trailed away as she realised, with a choking fury, that he'd done it to her again. He'd made her lie! She screwed up her face in anguish, then started to run again.

But in an instant he was in front of her, blocking her way. He caught hold of her arm with a biting ferocity. 'Oh, no! You're not going anywhere. You're coming with me and you're going to hear me out whether you like it or not!'

And with that he marched her back to the Range Rover, and swept her up in his arms. She struggled and fought, kicking her legs helplessly and hammering on his chest with her clenched fists. But she might just as well have saved her energy. His powerful build was quite equal to holding a struggling woman securely while still managing to open the car door. He almost threw her in to the passenger-seat, then locked her in before coming round to climb into the driver's seat.

He started the engine and eased the big vehicle out into the narrow streets of the town before giving voice to his cruel thoughts once more.

'So you cooked up your little plan, eh? You decided to give up your rights in law to see if you could wring an out-of-court settlement from me? No doubt you thought you could sting me for a good deal more than the value of the house? After all, you know perfectly well that I'm too immersed in my writing to want to get involved in a long, draining legal battle. And that I could afford to buy you off handsomely these days!'

Lizzy pressed her knotted fists into her cheeks. This was awful! What on earth had she done to make him think this of her? Her fury seethed away in the pit of her stomach, while her mind battled against incomprehending bewilderment.

'No!' she protested vehemently. 'How could you think that?'

But he seemed not to hear. The harsh note of his voice rang through the air. 'As it happens, my *notaire* also came up with a plan for resolving things out of court. But her plan was a good deal more generous than yours.

Equitable, even.' He stopped abruptly, letting the darkness and the silence fill the void between them.

'She suggested...' he said at length '...that we marry. A marriage of convenience, of course. This would establish our joint interest in the property afresh. Then we could divorce, with one or other of us buying out a half-interest when the time came. But of course, you wouldn't be interested in something as fair-minded as that, would you, Lizzy? You want every penny you can get your hands on, after all.'

'Of course I don't! How dare you suggest that I'm trying to rook you? Of course I want to be fair and generous—you don't have a monopoly on fine feelings, you know!'

'So you'll marry me, will you?' he sneered tauntingly. 'Or would it represent too big a financial loss on your own plan?'

'Of course I'll marry you!' she cried furiously. How dared he even suggest for one moment that she wouldn't?

CHAPTER SIX

THERE was only one thing to do, Lizzy decided after watching dawn sweep across the valley, filling it with a grainy blue mist before flooding the land with the drenched colours of Southern France. And that was to tell him that she had made a mistake. She had never heard anything so impossible in all her life as the idea of marrying him to get her hands on a half-share in the house. Especially as she'd decided she didn't want any kind of share in it now.

When she went downstairs he was already there, standing out on the terrace watching the summer sun swimming up into the sky.

'Nick?' She was unexpectedly nervous, speaking his name. Which Nick was she going to find? The difficult stranger she'd met when she first arrived, and whose company she had so missed these past few days? Or the ruthless, cynical man who'd got her so wrong the night before?

He turned to face her, leaning back against the low balustrade. His face was unreadable. Paler than usual, she thought, though that might just have been an effect of the dark stubble on his unshaved chin.

'Yes?'

'I've come to talk about last night.'

'Thinking better of it are you, now you've had time to run through your accounts?' There was no mistaking the acid timbre of his voice.

It had been a long night. She had tossed and turned through every moment of it, twisting their conversations around in her head, trying to view them from all angles in the hope she'd be able to understand why he had come to believe she was only out to wring money from him. Now his unkind words dug into her sharply. To her dismay her lower lip began to quiver and she found tears springing so copiously to her eyes that there was no chance of stemming them. She stumbled slightly, turning back towards the stairs. She'd just have to put this conversation on hold until she'd got herself under control.

But Nick had other ideas. He caught her wrist in his, gripping it tightly as she brushed past him.

'Are you going somewhere? Albi perhaps?' he asked sourly.

Oh, damn him! The venom in his voice brought her pride surging to the surface. She wasn't going to let him see how deeply he had hurt her. With a furious sniff she stemmed the tears, turning her pinched face to him.

'As far away from here as possible, as it happens!' she muttered through clenched teeth.

'Running out on our agreement, eh, Lizzy? Little Miss Honesty?'

'No!' She spat the word at him.

He didn't flinch. He just kept looking at her coldly, unemotionally, as if she had mutated from the person he ate meals with, laughed with, *had practically made love with*, for goodness' sake—into some species of reptile. Inside she floundered in a formless sea of bewilderment. But her chin went up defiantly. Her eyes met his determinedly. He could choose to think what he liked of her, but she would never, ever let him see that she cared.

'As it happens I'm going to my workshop. Today, in celebration of our engagement, I shall get out my wheel and make a few bowls.'

He dropped her wrist abruptly. His mouth curved into a sardonic smile. 'So that you'll have something to throw at me in moments of marital disharmony?'

'I wouldn't waste anything so precious,' she said haughtily, disarmed to find his mood so swiftly mellowing. 'Anyway, it's not going to be that sort of marriage.'

'Isn't it?' His voice was seductively low.

Lizzy's skin hugged her tight. The little hairs on the back of her neck stood on end. Now what on earth had he meant by that?

'This marriage...' she said deliberately '...is simply a ploy to ensure that we don't waste years of our lives in a pointless legal battle. Right?'

'Of course...' he agreed. But that smile was still hovering somewhere behind his eyes.

They travelled down to Montpellier for the simple civil ceremony, staying in a charming, small hotel in the medieval quarter of the historic town. They had separate rooms, of course.

Since Lizzy had made it plain that she was going to go through with the marriage, that sour edge had fled from Nick's manner. Unfortunately.

It made her realise how much the house must mean to him, and gave her the courage to go forward. It was the only way she could secure his interests, and she wasn't going to wriggle out of it. But the man she'd dined with, the one who accused her of scheming to wring money out of him, would have been a much healthier prospect as a husband. She scarcely found that man attractive at all.

Nick took her to the city's exciting modern shopping complex when they arrived. He insisted on buying her a lovely dress in green voile, sprigged with tiny white and yellow flowers. It was very floaty and very summery. And there was a wide-brimmed hat trimmed with little white and yellow flowers to go with it. He said they'd better look as if they meant business, or the authorities might suspect the marriage wasn't all it should be. He wore his cream linen suit.

It was blessedly anonymous, and Lizzy managed to keep her mind quite blank throughout the ceremony. All except the bit where he put a simple gold band on her finger. Her stomach flipped over then, but she soon got things back under control. Just as well it was all in French. It hadn't seemed like a proper wedding at all.

They drove straight back to Mon Abri.

'How do you feel, Mrs Holt?' he asked as the Range Rover wove its way through the narrow streets towards the road back home.

She stared at him from under the brim of the hat. In the days since she'd agreed to the marriage he'd resumed his relaxed air of ease. But his keen eyes, which had once surveyed her so wryly, rarely met hers at all. And his voice, when he spoke, had been desiccated. Now his voice was different. Warmer. With an underlying hum of that old, sardonic humour.

'You're in a good mood,' she muttered warily.

'That's right.'

Why should it surprise her? He'd secured his house. Of course he was happy. It was only she who was condemned to live for months on an emotional tightrope.

How long did it take to get a divorce in France, anyway?
She wished he'd go back to being nasty.

'You can afford to be, I suppose,' she sighed
despondently.

He was silent for a while. Then he said evenly, 'This
marriage was supposed to solve problems for both of
us. We own the house equally now, without having to
go to court to prove anything. It will be a while before
we can finally decide how to resolve matters. But until
we do, can I suggest that we call a truce?'

'Of course.' But her voice was still prickly. Then she
relented. It was hardly his fault that she still found it
unbearably arousing to be so near him. That was the
real problem, after all. That was at the root of her misery.

As the car sped north towards the misty line of mountains on the horizon she began to relax. The deed was
done. There was no going back. It was only now, as her
muscles gradually unknotted themselves, that she realised
how tense she had been for so long. The road stretched
out cleanly like a ribbon in front of them.

As the mountains grew closer, and the car began to
climb, her drifting thoughts began to tangle themselves
around an idea. A new idea. It began to dawn on Lizzy
that although Nick had claimed the marriage was the
fairest way of sorting things out for both of them, it was
actually a good deal fairer on her than it was on him.
He had really been rather generous as far as she was
concerned. After all, he hadn't believed her when she'd
said she no longer wanted the house.

With two bestsellers behind him, a third nearing com-
pletion and the worldwide television rights to his books
sold for some undisclosed sum—she remembered having
read that in the papers some months ago—he *could* have

afforded to handle his side of things with very little inconvenience to himself. He could, she supposed, have engaged a team of lawyers to scuttle between courts and Mon Abri in their gleaming limousines. And if things had started to look bad for him he could have offered her a very large sum of money to get her to drop her case. He'd made it plain that he thought that was what she was after in the first place.

She would have been the one trailing back and forth in her dusty van for years and years only to lose, or give up, in the end. But now her half-share was secure.

She took off her hat and sat it on her lap. Then she looked across at him. He was concentrating on his driving. Yes. He was being generous towards her after all. She let the sigh out slowly and silently, so that he wouldn't hear. She wished she hadn't figured that one out. She was very used to the idea that she was an unwelcome and meaningless intrusion on his life. It made it so much easier to keep her feelings at bay. Of course, she could be wrong. She'd never spoken to a lawyer herself about it all, after all. Maybe his lawyer had told him that his contract was absolutely useless? That she would be sure to win if ever they got near a court? But why then had he advised her from the start to get a lawyer of her own? That creeping tide of pleasure wouldn't go away. Those feelings of hers were rushing up to meet her all over again, and she felt as if she might drown.

'The wedding breakfast!' he said with a twisted attempt at a smile.

'Don't!' she winced. 'I really hate deception. Even when it *is* in a good cause.'

He popped the cork, letting the bottle fizz dramatically before filling her glass.

'Never mind. Drink this and then perhaps you won't feel so bad about it. Look upon the champagne as a celebration of our cleverness in finding a simple solution to a very tangled problem.'

She sipped at her glass, then gave him a broad grin. 'It's a good job Grandma didn't leave the house to my brother. You couldn't have taken the easy option, then!'

He laughed. Those two deep lines appeared in his cheeks, signalling the return of genuine mirth.

They both laughed, letting themselves slide into the effervescent good humour that had so often characterised their shared meals here on the terrace. It wasn't until they were well into their second glasses that the sound of a car engine negotiating the track disturbed their mood.

'You stay here,' groaned Nick. 'I'll go round to the front and head whoever it is off. It's probably someone from the village. I won't be a minute.'

But when he returned he wasn't alone. There were two other people marching around the house with him. And at the sight of them Lizzy almost dropped her glass. Only the fact that a death-like rigour clamped her fingers to the stem saved the beautiful crystal flute from shattering into smithereens.

'Elizabeth! What on earth is going on?' Her mother's small mouth was tightly pursed, her eyes glittering beneath her severely plucked eyebrows.

'Mother! What in the world are you doing here?'

'Daddy and I decided to come over here for a quiet holiday. And not a moment too soon, by the look of things. It seems you've wasted no time in making a sordid love-nest out of my mother's house!'

Lizzy gaped. What a typically vile thing for them to assume! And how *could* they have just descended like this without warning her? Never once in the seven years since she had left to go to college had they ever visited her—announced or otherwise. Until now.

'This is not a love-nest! Honestly, you sound like one of those awful Sunday tabloids which you profess to despise! And it's no longer Grandma's house. It's mine!'

Monica Braithewaite tucked her chin firmly into the plump folds of her neck, and turned coldly to her husband. 'You tell her, Ronald...' she ordered snidely.

He gave his wife a smile of complicity. 'Doesn't look like it is yours, Elizabeth,' he barked. 'The probate chappie turned up trumps. Explained that the laws of inheritance in France are different from those in Britain. He reckons you'll never get the bequest to stick over here. Reckons we can consider it *ours*.'

'That's right, Elizabeth,' cut in her mother. 'I never thought I'd live to see the day when I admitted that the French could improve upon British justice, but in this case...' she turned a sickly-sweet smile on her daughter, blinking fast '...it seems I was wrong.'

'Mother,' she said furiously, 'how could you come out here like this? How could you just appear, behaving as if the place was yours already—without even warning me? We're happy here... It isn't fair!'

But Nick had stepped forward. His left arm came protectively around Lizzy's shoulder, while he offered his right hand to Monica Braithewaite.

'Let me introduce myself. I'm Nicholas Holt.' His eyes were fixed steadfastly on Lizzy's mother.

She fixed him back with her pale, glittering blue eyes. Nick didn't waver, simply thrust his hand a little nearer, so that she was forced to take it. He pumped her hand furiously, then offered it to her father, keeping Lizzy at his side all the while.

'We're delighted to see you, aren't we, Lizzy?' he asked, his voice strong and confident. She glanced up at him in bewilderment. Just when she thought she was getting the measure of him he went and did something which knocked her sideways.

'You see,' he was explaining genially, his face warmed by a smile, 'Lizzy and I got married this morning. Normally it would be a family occasion, but as both our families were so far away we decided to get married quietly here, and then perhaps have a big church ceremony at a later date in England.' And he even produced the marriage certificate from his jacket pocket, and presented it proudly for their inspection.

Lizzy gulped. Why on earth had he decided to go and tell them that they were married? Let alone making it look as if it were the real thing! Surely he couldn't *like* them? But if not, why on earth was he trying to ingratiate himself with them in this way?

He turned to Lizzy's father. 'So why don't I pour you a glass of champagne each, and you can toast our future happiness? And then I can see about getting you fixed up in a hotel for the night.'

'Elizabeth! This is preposterous!' her mother's voice was small and choked, her eyes small and angry. Then she turned on Nick. 'I think I should remind you, Mr Holt——'

But Nick ignored her, interrupting cheerfully, 'Oh, do call me Nick! After all, I'm one of the family, now, aren't I? And perhaps I can call you Mona and Ron?'

He was play-acting! The urge to laugh was mounting fast. Lizzy bit her lip so hard that her eyes watered.

He didn't wait for the negative response that she could see springing to their lips, but continued breezily, 'Do sit down. The glasses are on the dresser in the kitchen, Mona. You should be able to find them without any difficulty.'

Lizzy had never before met anyone who had managed to get the better of her parents. But her mother trotted quite obediently—if resentfully—into the house. Nick seemed to have succeeded where the rest of the world had failed. He ushered her father into a seat. Then he sat down himself, pulling Lizzy—to her unadulterated horror—affectionately on to his lap.

'You'll excuse, us, won't you?' he grinned, nibbling at Lizzy's ear. 'But this *is* our wedding day. We were expecting a little peace and quiet, weren't we, darling?' And with that he picked up Lizzy's hand and began to kiss the tips of her fingers.

Lizzy risked a covert glance in the direction of her father. He looked as if he might have an apoplectic fit at any minute!

'Ah, Mona! You found them. Excellent. Do help yourselves...I was just telling Ron here that we're honeymooning at home. So you'll quite understand that it won't be possible to stay here for your holiday, won't you?'

But a triumphant gleam had entered her mother's eye. She was obviously re-garnering her strength. Lizzy turned her face to Nick's shoulder to hide a smile. Round one to him. But the bout was not over yet.

'I'm afraid you failed to understand my husband's point earlier. This house is not Elizabeth's. I can't imagine how much money the pair of you have squandered on getting the house tarted up so quickly...' she blinked furiously, pursing her mouth into a simpering smile '...but I'm afraid it's been money down the drain.'

Nick tilted his head to one side. 'I certainly heard his remarks on the matter. And I think the solicitor's comments may well be valid. The law of inheritance is quite explicit and certainly different here in France.'

Now what was Nick saying? He seemed to be conceding defeat on her behalf. She raised her head, and looked belligerently at her mother.

Nick squeezed her shoulder warningly. 'Be that as it may, the fact still remains that we are newly married.'

Why wasn't he telling them that he'd bought the house from Grandpa? That surely should have silenced their objections far more effectively? Lizzy decided to hold her tongue. Whatever his reasoning, he seemed to be managing to make them do pretty much what he wanted. Whereas she'd never once succeeded, in all her twenty-four years. She might as well give him the floor and see what he managed to achieve.

'There's nowhere nearby for us to stay,' complained her mother coldly and decisively. 'And anyway, I can't see that our presence will make much difference. After all, young people nowadays don't wait...' She sucked in her cheeks, refraining from completing the remark, but only too aware that its implication must be understood.

'You can be in Albi within forty minutes,' Nick responded evenly. But there was an underlying note of danger in his voice. It was clear he would brook no argument. 'There are several very good hotels there.'

'We *can't* leave, as it happens,' smirked Monica, her voice a triumphant whine. 'A tractor's overturned on the track. We're blocked in.'

Nick surveyed her with icy disbelief. 'A tractor? How on earth?'

'Bloody French drivers,' muttered her father disdainfully. 'Creeping up the hill like a snail. We were stuck behind it for miles. Finally manage to overtake, and the stupid man swerves into a ditch. The thing just went over sideways. Got what was coming to him if you ask me. A big car like ours doesn't like to be shackled by a machine like that!'

'But the driver?' Nick's voice was riddled with scorn.

'Oh, dear me!' blinked her mother. 'The least said about him, the better! He was jolly lucky. Not even a scratch! But instead of being grateful the horrid man was most rude. Thank goodness we don't speak French!'

Lizzy had been listening with mounting disbelief. Normally, by this point, she would have been flying at her parents with clenched fists, white with rage. But, oddly, she felt as if she'd been watching them from a distance. Cut off. As if their loathsome manners couldn't touch her for once.

It was Nick whose voice came, laced with disgust. 'Perhaps it's as well there's no accommodation in the village. The local people might have worried that you'd be embarrassed when they turned you away. They're normally so hospitable. But not fools.'

He tipped Lizzy gently off his lap, then pulled her affectionately against him so that she could hear each beat of his steady heart. He ran his lips lightly over the top of her head before speaking again.

'Now, I think my wife could do with a rest, couldn't you, darling? Why don't you pop up to our room and lie down for an hour? I shall take care of your parents!'

He turned and gave Lizzy a slow, burning smile. His eyes were so laden with passion that it seemed that at any moment he must pull her to him and kiss her. He didn't take his eyes off her for a moment. A delicious pleasure oozed inside her. She wished this pretence could go on for ever!

He led her firmly indoors to the foot of the stairs. As soon as they were out of her parents' hearing she turned to congratulate him. But to her astonishment, the eyes which had been devouring hers with such a burning intensity were cold with anger.

'Nick?'

'How could you, Lizzy?' His words were muffled with a choking fury.

She was shocked. 'How could I what?' she breathed, uncomprehending.

'They're monsters! I refuse to believe that they're part of the human race! And yet, apart from the odd little joke, you never once said *anything* ... You've told me so much about your grandparents... But your own parents? How could you *protect* them like that?' He looked at her with a deep and penetrating disdain.

'But it wasn't them I was protecting!' she cried, so appalled by his disgust that she blurted out the long-hidden truth. 'Don't you see, Nick? Don't you understand? I wasn't protecting *them*... It was never them...'

She didn't wait for his response, but simply turned and thundered up the staircase to her room. She slammed the door hard, and turned the key with shaking fingers. She had no idea whether or not he had followed her— probably not, if the look of unmitigated loathing on his face was anything to go by. But she felt naked and ashamed. She had to hide.

She hid in the shower, almost shearing the buttons off her dress in her haste to bury herself in the cleansing water. She turned it on full blast, and let the torrents gush over her, running through her thick curls, streaming into her eyes, cascading over every inch of her body. And all the while she held in her mind's eye the vision of his face, his lips curled with distaste, as if the very sight of her made him feel sick.

He'd played out an elaborate charade just minutes before. He'd looked at her then as if he wanted her...was proud of her...as if he truly loved her. But that had just been a mask, worn so that he could triumph over her parents.

Lizzy recalled the temptation to dissemble she herself had known over the years. It would have been so easy to pretend that she was the daughter they wanted, instead of the one they had. At first to get their attention...their approval. Later, when she had accepted the truth, to avoid the incessant criticism. But she'd fought the temptation away. Far rather, she had told herself, their hatred honestly earned, than their love won by a lie.

She frowned, sluicing the water off her face with her hands. But Nick hadn't played the part in order to win their approval. In fact, he hadn't seemed to care much what they thought of him. He'd wanted them to go, certainly. But he could have achieved that in far grander style simply by telling them that he'd bought the house from Grandpa. When he had cast his arms about her, when he had told them with all the appearance of honest pride that they were married, he had been deceiving them in order to... in order to protect *her*.

And she had felt protected, enfolded in his arms. It was then that she had stopped battling with them in her heart, if only for a while. It was only then that she had felt she could watch their pathetic spite with detachment. Nick had made it all right for her. For the first time in her life the hurt had gone away. Because she was proud to be thought Nick's wife. Proud to be thought beloved by him. Proud to be seen to love him in return.

She stepped blindly out of the shower and, without bothering to dry herself, went to sit in front of the dressing-table.

Her face in the mirror was palest ivory. Her eyes were huge and round. Her wet hair clung like seaweed to her shoulders. Her damp skin prickled. The charade was over now... but her feelings lived on. Sitting there on his lap she had thought she was merely pretending to love him. But she had been wrong. She shivered. Because she really did love Nick Holt. Despite all her vows, she was deeply and desperately in love with him.

She groaned as if in pain. It couldn't be true? Surely? But there was no denying the knowledge. Her mind opened to it, like thunderclouds peeling back to reveal the honest blue of the sky beyond. She, Lizzy Braithewaite, had fallen in love with Nicholas Holt. While he...? The image of his face, marked with disdain, again swam before her eyes.

Of course it was wildly hurtful to know that he loathed her so. She wouldn't be human if she didn't ache to have him love her in return. But really, when you thought about it, it was just as well. It wasn't in her nature to make love work. She would end by ruining everything. This way there would be nothing to spoil—no one to hurt. It was much, much better like this.

She dried herself hastily, scrambled back into her dress, and towelled her hair furiously this time before tying it safely into a top-knot. The sooner she got back down there the better. She needed to show him that, however unkind her parents might be towards her, she could still get her act together. Whatever else she had lost, she still had her pride.

CHAPTER SEVEN

LIZZY was halfway down the stairs before she heard the voices. Nick was talking in low, authoritative tones, and it was difficult to make out his words. Her father's gruff bark, however, was easier to distinguish.

Suddenly she was petrified of confronting Nick. Was it written on her face? Would he know how she felt? And yet if she went running back upstairs he would think she was cowed by those ghastly parents of hers. Or worse—by him... She took a deep breath and continued her descent. At least the prospect of facing her parents wasn't bothering her at all.

The air in the room seemed to shiver as he strode in through the french doors. The staircase, with its open, carved rails, led directly into the room. There was nowhere to hide.

His eyes went straight to her. She thought she had seen him angry several times. Not the least just half an hour since when the expression in his eyes alone had sent her fleeing to her room. But now when she looked into his face she knew she had never encountered the real depths of his anger before. His skin had darkened ominously, his lips were a rigid, white line and his eyes granite-black.

'What the hell...?' he growled at her from the depths of his throat. He paused. Then he made a slight dismissive movement of his head. 'Get back upstairs. Now.

And pack a change of warm clothes. Then stay in your room until I come for you.'

She obeyed unquestioningly. It was only when she had stuffed a warm sweater, jeans and woolly socks into a lightweight yellow holdall that she stopped to wonder what was going on.

He came up to fetch her, his face still thunderous. As she obeyed his silent gesture to leave her room, the holdall slung over her shoulder, he produced a bunch of keys from his pocket and locked her door behind him.

'That's one room they won't be able to stick their prying noses into,' he muttered with satisfaction. Then he proceeded to lock his study, adding, 'And that's another.'

He took the holdall from her and held her firmly by the arm as they went downstairs. Although he said nothing, the pressure of his fingers curling around her elbow let her know in no uncertain terms that he was in control of the situation, and she was to do or say nothing that would challenge him.

Her parents must still have been on the terrace, because there was no sign of them as they made their way to the door. Nick stopped to gather up a colourful Afghan from the back of one of the sofas. He slung it over his shoulder, then picked up a canvas bag from beside the door.

Once outside she looked up at him and asked, 'What's going on?'

He didn't bother to turn his grim face towards her. He merely muttered coldly, 'We're off to continue our nuptial celebrations where the air is less polluted.' He began to walk away from the house.

So that was what it was all about... Having embarked upon the pretence of a honeymoon, he was bound to carry it through. And presumably he had no intention of sharing his bedroom with her for a make-believe night of passion. She was being taken along as a vital prop, without which the illusion would crumble.

'Come on,' he glowered, gripping her arm even more fiercely.

'But where are we going? You can't just march me off like this!' She felt free to protest now that they were out of earshot of her family.

He pulled up short, jolting her to a halt before loosing her arm. 'You're free to go back in there with them, if that's what you want!'

'Of course I don't!' she muttered. 'I only wanted to know where we were going.'

She felt stupidly hurt by the harsh light in his eyes when he looked at her. Her throat tightened with emotion every time she glanced up at him. Her love wanted to cry itself aloud... Even when he looked at her so coldly, a yearning ache would rise up in her chest, making her hold her breath for a short moment. Oh, how it hurt to have him loathe her so... And the hurt, she knew, was not going to go away.

She had no illusions about her ability to fall out of love with him, now—or ever, probably. She could try, but she knew with a deadly certainty that it wasn't going to work. Before she had opened her mind to the truth, she had tried to be pleased when he was annoyed with her. She had thought it made her own emotions more secure. Now there was no fooling herself. She wanted him to love her in return. Or at least to tease her and offer her those devastating, dry smiles. Now that she didn't even have that, she felt numbingly bereft.

His strides beat out a thundering tattoo on the dry ground. He was ignoring her.

Her ragged emotions couldn't bear the silence. 'I'm sorry they've annoyed you so much,' she said bleakly.

He still didn't look at her. '*They* haven't annoyed me at all.'

So it *was* her. She was the one who was painting his features dark with disdain. She bit hard on the tip of her tongue.

He was walking at an impressive speed. She had to half run to keep up with him. They were following the winding sheep-track behind the house, climbing upwards into the mountains.

'Are we going to the shepherd's hut?' she gasped eventually, when she began to recognise the route.

'Got it in one,' he responded sourly. 'The only hotel for miles around which doesn't involve going *down* the road.'

'But...' She knew he wasn't going to like what she had to say. She didn't much care. He didn't like anything she said, anyway. 'There's a problem. The thing is, Nick——'

'For God's sake stop whining. You can always go back down there to the loving bosom of your family if you'd prefer.'

She swallowed hard. 'Nick, I'm hungry. If we're going to stay there all night I think I'll starve.'

'You know the answer,' he replied acidly. 'Go back. They'll probably have laid on a surprise party for you, with a running buffet and a three-tiered cake with a silver horseshoe on the top.'

She smarted at the gibe. What was it he'd said? That he couldn't bear the way she'd tried to protect them? She'd tried to explain, but had he understood? It wasn't them that she protected by her silence, but herself. Her pride. She couldn't bear people to know how insensitive and cruel they could be. She dreaded the thought that people might assume that she must be a little like them. It had happened once or twice. Out with them, in the street, or on holiday. They would bray out their beastly arrogance and people would squirm and withdraw. Lizzy had been with them. Their child. She had seen the revulsion in people's eyes. And had felt all the humiliation of being taken for one of them.

She looked up at Nick. His eyes were set on the distant horizon. His jaw was thrust forward, his hands stuffed deep into his trouser pockets. With the holdall and the colourful rug slung carelessly over his broad shoulder he looked strangely like some ancient explorer, searching for a new world. He also still looked furious.

She sighed, struggling to make up the few steps which separated them. No matter how fast she scrambled, he was always a stride or two ahead. She could have asked him to slow down or to wait. But that would have been tantamount to asking for his pity. And that was another commodity she could well do without. She didn't need it and she didn't want it and it was anything but appropriate.

Her parents had once asked a classmate to stay during the school holidays. While she was there her parents had put up a good front, but it hadn't been enough to deceive the astute Fiona. Back at school she had told the whole class how mean poor Lizzy's parents were to her. The girls were young and warm-hearted. They had only

meant to be kind. But they had kept on offering Lizzy
bits of chocolate, as if she were a sick dog in need of
consolation. And they had patted her shoulder through
her thin school cardigan all the time, too. In the end she
came to suspect that they would have had her put down
if the opportunity had arisen, to save her from what they
assumed to be her suffering.

Lizzy was too proud to acknowledge their sympathy.
It would have meant admitting there might be some
cause. So she had put up with their sympathetic handling
for a whole term, before finally losing her temper with
one particularly tender-hearted girl. She should have
done it sooner. With the fickleness of youth, the class
had swiftly turned to knitting squares for charity instead.

The inside of the hut was gloomy. It had a beaten earth
floor, a single table and an upright chair, a cupboard,
a solitary, narrow wooden bed and a hearth with a hob.
There was no electricity, and no logs in the hearth.

'I thought you told me this was a refuge for travellers?' queried Lizzy. 'They'd freeze in winter if they
ended up here!'

'The shepherd brings what he needs when he comes.
Then the villagers make sure there is some fuel here,
when the weather gets cold,' said Nick, opening the
cupboard.

Lizzy wandered over to examine the bed. She tested
the mattress, which was covered by a thin grey blanket.
The mattress gave stiffly beneath her hand, and stayed
dented. She lifted the corner of the blanket to examine
it. It was a sort of brown canvas bag, obviously filled
with something which had lost its zest for life. She

punched at it with her fist. A cloud of dust rose up. Now there was an even bigger dent.

'This bed is pretty grim,' she stated tiredly.

Nick turned to face her. He had found a hurricane lamp and candles in the cupboard and was busily setting them out on the table.

'It's a palliasse.' He came across the room to examine it. 'Left over from the first war, no doubt. It should be filled with something soft, though.' And he lifted his hand and slapped it hard. The cloud of dust he produced was enough to set Lizzy sneezing, and the hearty thump had almost flattened the wretched thing. He opened the fastenings at one corner and examined the contents.

'Heather, I think,' he muttered with a sigh of irritation. 'But whatever it once was, it's mostly dust now.'

'Ugh!' exclaimed Lizzy. 'It'll be like sleeping on a compost heap.'

He eyed her balefully. 'You can always chicken out,' he said in a desiccated voice.

She felt her colour mounting, and sensed the adrenalin beginning to course through her veins. She had had about as much as she could take for one day.

'Stop it!' she demanded. 'You can dislike me as much as you want. But please do me the courtesy of disliking me for my own self. I refuse to be lumped together with...with *them*!' And with a sweeping gesture she pointed angrily towards Mon Abri.

He shrugged insolently. 'And what makes you think I don't dislike you for your own self, Lizzy?'

She felt her skin positively flame. 'I'm sure you do. But you were laughing with me when they arrived. And you were drinking champagne with me. And at least you were pretending that we weren't sworn enemies. We both were. It was, at least, civilised. Only now that you think you've got the measure of me you can't see the point of keeping up the pretence, can you?'

He folded his arms and stood watching her. Oh, damn him! It was always the same with him. She'd lose her temper and he'd just get calmer. And colder. As if the fire which fuelled her froze him solid.

Her fury roared up again, unassuaged.

'Damn you, Nicholas Holt!' Her voice had risen into a fierce cry. 'I will *not* be judged by my family! I will not! They shoved me into the arms of a nanny when I was a few days old, and it was the best day's work they ever did as far as I'm concerned. And in case you think I was a deprived child, let me add that she was a very loving nanny, and she took me often to see my very loving grandparents, and she made sure I was sent to a school with very loving housemistresses. So I did remarkably well for myself. Especially when you consider the alternative. So don't you dare ever, for one moment, suggest that I'm like them!'

Suddenly he had lost what was left of his temper, too. 'Don't be so stupid, Lizzy! Of course I don't think you're like them!' His voice roared out so loudly that the small, dirty windowpane trembled in its frame. 'That...' he shouted bitterly '...is the problem.'

She glared at him in furious confusion. 'And what exactly is that supposed to mean?'

He turned his back on her, hunched his shoulders and went to stare out of the little window. 'Just forget it, eh, Lizzy?' he said sourly.

But she couldn't leave it alone. Exhaustion, the events of the day, the anguish of discovering that she had been reckless enough to fall in love with him, all tumbled together in a frantic storm of emotion.

'Forget it? Forget what? Forget the fact that earlier today you suggested calling a truce? Before *they* arrived we were getting on together perfectly well. And now you can't even bring yourself to look at me. The only conclusion I can draw is that you think I'm a party to their vile behaviour. Perhaps you even think that I asked them out here specifically to insult you. Is that it?'

His response was to spin on his heel, take a couple of swift paces across the room to where she was standing, catch hold of her shoulders and force his mouth hard upon hers.

She was shocked by the power of him. And with a inner cry of despair she knew that this time, angry though he was, she had no will left with which to resist. Whether he loved her or not didn't matter. Even the fact that he was so furious with her didn't count for anything. She loved him. This time she would not be able to pull away.

The kiss was fierce. His fingers bit into her shoulders through the thin voile of the floaty, summery dress. His tongue forced itself past her lips, her teeth, so that their mouths were quickly one, each exploring the passion of the other with a hard, questing motion. His teeth cut hard against her parted lips. The fierceness of him aroused her with a dramatic speed so that her own tongue darted out to explore his mouth with unleashed ardour. When he sensed that she was giving to him, not fighting, the muscles of his fingers unknotted themselves, and his hands flattened caressingly against her shoulders.

She looped her arms behind his neck, running her fingers through his hair, drawing his head closer to her own. With a tangible surge of emotion he pulled her to

him in a bear-hug which almost drove the breath from
her body. He dragged his mouth free, breathing raggedly
into her hair before he asked, 'Lizzy?'

She didn't reply. She couldn't admit with words that
she was his. But her silence, the clinging certainty of her
body crushed against him was answer enough.

He began to kiss her again. This time with all the tan-
talising delicacy she had tasted before. His arousal was
unbearably swift—matching her own unconstrained
passion. Standing in the dim, dusty room, their bodies
moulded fast to one another, she felt the hardness of
him against her and thrilled to the pressure. She rocked
against him as he let his mouth rove over her cheeks,
her brow, her eyes.

At last he broke free again, this time loosing his hold
with one arm to gather up the thick rug. Then, keeping
her tucked beneath the shelter of his arm, he led her out
into the mellow evening sunlight. He spread the rug on
the ground, and, taking her by the shoulders, sat her
down in the centre of it. He took off his jacket—the
cream linen creased and marked—and flung it aside.
Then he came down beside her, his fingers reaching out
to trace her profile. She shivered at the touch, aching
only to fold herself close to him once more, to feel the
hard, muscular planes of his body beneath her hands,
to know the pulse of answered desire.

But he took his time. He unfastened her hair—long
since dried by the warmth of the sun—letting it spill in
tousled glory on to her shoulders, so that it framed her
pleading face with a halo of burnished colour. His deft
fingers turned to the tiny buttons fastening the front of
her dress, opening them slowly one by one as the yearning
mounted demandingly inside Lizzy. Only when he had

pulled the dress from her, and discarded his shirt, did he take her in his arms again, and begin to kiss her with a new, restrained passion.

And all the while he had been undressing her his eyes had held no trace of his former anger. There was no distaste in the gaze that devoured her now. Only unalloyed, smouldering desire, so undisguised, so blatant that she shuddered with delight under his scrutiny.

When they had chosen the dress she had picked out a camisole and matching briefs in a fine aquamarine silk trimmed with white lace to wear beneath it. At the time it had been her secret—a silly impulsive desire to mark the day with bridal silk next to her skin. Now his hands slid easily over its satiny surface, revealing all the secrets beneath.

She ached to know again the sharp, sweet heat of his mouth on her breasts. She arched against him, thrusting their rounded fullness against the prickling hairs of his chest. His hand came round to caress them, plucking at the nipple beneath the silk until she cried out. And then his restraint fled, and his mouth scoured the silk, nudging the lace aside with his firm lips until the proud pale pink buds were revealed, bursting against his mouth.

There was no containing the urgency of their desire now. Time and again she moaned out her need as her hands dug demandingly into the solid muscle beneath his skin. And his mouth, his hands, stroked and caressed and massaged and kneaded her flesh, stripping her free of the fragile silk until her charged arousal drove her fingers to push desperately at the waistband of his trousers. He tore himself free of all his clothes then, his breath quaking with hard unslaked lust during the painful hiatus, and came to her in all his male splendour.

The white band of skin, where the sun had not reached, blazed against the dark shadow of his maleness. Her arms reached out to him and fiercely, wantonly, they held each other, clamouring against each other until, with a sharp stab of pain, he was moving in that deep, velvet place which existed only for him. She cried out her pain into the clear mountain air, turning her head to one side to free the hurt. He hesitated, was still for a moment, and then with groan he thrust against her, time and again, murmuring her name ... beyond reason, beyond control, tumbling headlong into the void of pleasure.

When at last he pulled free from her, there was no hesitation. His hand came swiftly down, his fingers trembling, to stroke away the pain. His mouth nuzzled against her breast, his tongue teasing the nipple which ached for his touch. And all the while his fingers caressed her. He was carrying her on a tide of sensation. She was coursing so sweetly, so powerfully, so purposefully that she gasped out a wail of bewildered pleasure before the massing sensations collided, sending her spinning off into that black, seamless well of delight where he had been, and which she entered with a grateful, shuddering cry of release.

Her face was against his chest. She tasted his sweat on her lips, felt the thud of his heart beneath his ribs. Felt tears wet on her cheeks. He raised himself up on to one elbow, and kissed her face, taking the salt tears away with the tip of his tongue.

'Oh, Lizzy...' he groaned, his voice immeasurably tender. 'Why didn't you tell me? If I'd only known it was your first time...'

But she shook her head, burying her face shyly in his skin. 'It was perfect…' she breathed. 'You couldn't have made it better than it was.'

He was silent. But his arms curved round her, pillowing her, protecting her. There was no place for words. They lay back for a long time, quietly, watching the sky. Dusk had gathered while they had made love. The blue firmament was dimmed, the light all concentrated on the western horizon. Lizzy shivered. It was beginning to get cold.

Nick turned to her. 'Beautiful though it is lying here while the sun sets, I must get the hurricane lamp going while daylight holds. Or it'll be too dark to see what I'm doing.'

She nodded her understanding, watching his big, lithe body as he got to his feet and walked, naked into the hut. He was beautiful. And she was happy that she had made love with him. It would be hard, going forward from this moment. Hard knowing that she loved him without being loved in return. But she was glad that once, at least, she had been able to describe her love with her mouth, her hands, her whole body, in the wordless song they had sung together.

She needed her warm clothes now. She was getting very cold. And there was a long night to endure before they could slip back into the shelter of their house, and take up the lives that they had shared for so long. She winced, wondering whether Nick would expect her to share his bed from now on. How could she say no, having once tasted this ecstasy? And yet how could she hide her love for him, nightly between the sheets? She hugged her arms around herself. He had taken her in lust. She had satisfied his carnal need. But he had been furious with her. His entire relationship with her was based on his need to hold on to his house. And, ultimately, his solitude.

She grimaced, forcing her mind to close on all her churning thoughts. This was neither a beginning nor an end. She would look neither forward nor back. She had made love with Nick, and when he came out of the hut he would, she knew, gather her once again into his arms, and speak to her tenderly. For this night at least there would be no future, no past. Only this moment, this now. And she would relish it for ever and ever.

He came out warmly dressed and bearing the lamp in one hand and the holdall in the other. She scrambled gratefully into her clothes, both loving and hating the idea that he was gazing on her nakedness.

'Look,' he said, extracting a tin from the bag. 'Biscuits. They were in the cupboard. At least we won't starve.'

They ate the biscuits as the last glimmer of daylight faded from the sky.

'Where shall we sleep?' asked Lizzy tentatively at last.

Nick sighed. 'That bed is out of the question. And I'm thirsty. There's no water here. Do you feel up to a hike, Lizzy? In the dark?'

CHAPTER EIGHT

THEY awoke together, a little after dawn. There had been blankets stowed in the cupboard of the hut, and together with the Afghan they made a cosy bed on the grass beside the pool. Curled close against Nick for warmth, both of them still wearing their sweaters and trousers and socks, Lizzy had slept soundly all night. She had felt blissfully tired after the strange and wonderful experience of walking through the night, in the crook of Nick's arm, with just the hurricane lamp for light.

His grey eyes were fixed on the dancing leaves of the branches overhead. She watched him through half-closed lids, stretched out comfortably beneath the blankets. His features were in repose, his lips curving into a hint of a smile. If only life could stand still, she thought wonderingly, then I should be certain of happiness forever.

He turned to face her. 'You're awake?' he commented.

She nodded.

A broad, lazy smile spread itself across his face. 'Swing the waterfall with me Lizzy? Naked, at dawn? It will be wonderful, I promise...'

Her heart leapt with delight. But almost immediately her eyes clouded. She ought to draw back now. She knew it. Before it was too late. 'I...I don't know. I don't think so...'

141

He was silent for a very long time, his eyes returning to the pattern of the leaves against the sky. Then he turned his head towards her and ran his thumb lightly down her cheek, following the curve of her jaw. 'Come on, Lizzy? Last night there was pain...I want you to know how it *can* be...'

It was no good. She should have known how impossible it would be ever to refuse him, now that the die was cast. Slowly she sat up and pulled her jersey over her head.

The water was screamingly cold. The sight of him, charging headlong into the depths, plunging beneath its silver surface before emerging to slice through it to the beach beyond, stirred and invigorated her. He was so wonderfully...beautifully...*grandly* male. And she loved him so. There *were* no tomorrows, she reminded herself fiercely. Only this deep and honest love that *would* have its way. Joyously she set free her doubts and followed him, gasping at the tingling coldness of the water against her naked skin. On the far side he pulled her to him with one hand as he grabbed the rope.

'Hold tight to me,' he ordered. She clung fast to his neck as he clambered on to the branch. Then one powerful arm grasped her tight, as, headily, together, they swung out across the pool and right through the tumbling sheet of water to the safety of the ledge beyond. This time there was no attempt to disguise his arousal. He kissed her hard, before telling her to hold tight once more. She clung to him with her legs as well as her arms as back they went, exhilarated and charged with desire, through the waterfall to the small beach, where they fell together, warmed by passion, a tangled mass of arms and legs, white and brown.

They chafed each other with their kisses, till the blood roared hot in their veins. Then they made love, with a bursting, urgent ferocity, on the little beach at the water's edge. And this time, together, limbs entwined, they crashed through the cascade of surging desire, to the joy of a simultaneous release.

For sweet minutes together they lay, languid and replete, tangled in each other's arms. The air moved over their skin, raising Lizzy's pink nipples into tight, prominent peaks.

'Mmmm...' murmured Nick, observing them through drowsy eyes. 'Delicious. You're making me hungry again...'

A radiant happiness burst open inside Lizzy's heart. She loved him. Oh, how she loved him! And here she was, lying curled against his side, in one of the most beautiful places on earth. And he was looking at her so enticingly, so luxuriously, as if the needs of his flesh, his desire for her, had obliterated every other emotion he had ever felt. It was enough, after all. To be wanted by him, to rouse the animal in him, was enough. She listened to his heart beat steadily beneath his ribs and allowed herself to be glad.

He stretched, then sat up, his fingers travelling lightly across her breasts and down over her ribs to lie softly on the curve of her hip. Then he knelt beside her, and, running his lips over her face, he proceeded to gather

her up into his arms. When his hands had slipped securely beneath her shoulders and knees, he stood up, swinging her with him, so that her cheek came to lie against his naked shoulder.

He stepped out into the shallow edge of the water.

'What are you doing?' she murmured, mildly puzzled, but too blissfully happy to care.

'I'm carrying you across the threshold of our universe,' he teased.

She looked up into his face. His grey eyes were fastened on hers. Her lower lip shook almost perceptibly as heady emotion piled up within her. At any moment she might cry for the sheer wonder of it all. She swallowed hard.

'Actually, Mrs Holt,' he continued, mockery glinting in his bright eyes, 'all I'm really doing is trying to keep you warm and dry while I carry you back to our lovenest. I want to make love with you all over again, you see. And I've got a feeling we'll both enjoy it more if you're not clammy and shivering.'

She laughed, then snuggled her face into the silken pillow of his skin, planting little kisses on his shoulder... the ridge of his collarbone... his neck.

He walked confidently, thigh-deep in the sparkling water, around the border of the pool until he reached the grassy verge on the far side. Then he crossed to the pile of tumbled blankets and clothes and laid her reverently down. Her calves brushed across his powerful, muscular thighs, the dark hairs plastered close to his burnished skin. His skin was cold to the touch. She pulled the blankets around them both, until they were securely covered against the cool brush of the fresh morning air. And then she lay back and waited for his mouth to claim hers.

She was not disappointed. He kissed her delicately, tantalisingly, his lips nibbling against hers, the tip of his tongue tracing the contours of her mouth. And then he pulled back, and watched her face as he ran his fingers, feather-light and dancing over her shoulders and on to her breasts. She felt her eyes widen as his thumb brushed against her nipple, and then, wantonly, she arched her back and closed her eyes and succumbed to every delightful sensation his body could provide for hers.

This time she allowed instinct to possess her entirely. When her lips longed to brush against the springy hairs of his chest, she tore her head away from his mouth and gently lowered her swollen, parted lips to his breast. And when his flat, dark nipples lay against her cheek she rounded on them, amazed to see them respond to the flicker of her tongue. Her hands plied his flesh as his plied hers. Her palms flattened against his broad back, then clutched at the packed muscle beneath the skin as wild desire overwhelmed her. He possessed her slowly, lingeringly, and then, when the force of sensation drove restraint away, with all the raw male power that stirred her so deeply.

She was his. He was hers. Not in the fantasy of teenage dreams, but in this real nest of blankets, sheltered from the sharp mountain air. If he could want her like this, if he could just smile and laugh and not balk at her staying, then she would school herself to believe it enough.

Afterwards, they lay curled against one another, watching the leaves against the sky while the sun rose higher and higher.

Her mind drifted aimlessly, wandering back to remember the calm of sitting on his lap, while her parents shrank into cardboard figures, with no more power to hurt her than forgotten dreams.

'Did you really know,' she asked idly, 'that my parents might be entitled to the house?'

He shifted his arm behind her neck, and pulled away slightly. 'Yes,' he conceded.

'Then why didn't you tell me?'

There was another pause. 'There are a lot of ifs and buts and maybes. It was just another of those endless legal complications I mentioned. And very far from certain. There didn't seem to be any point.'

She was the one to fall silent now. Until at last she asked, 'If you knew it might not even be my house, then why did you marry me?'

In her heart she knew the answer she wanted to hear. She was also realistic enough to know she wasn't going to get it. She must learn not to ask questions like that, or he'd start to feel hounded.

'Work it out...' he said, with that faint hint of mockery which set her heart jumping. At least he hadn't said anything scathing...yet...

'I'm sure you can come up with a reason if you put your busy, little brain to it, Lizzy!'

He was teasing her. Now *that* was right! She smiled. 'My brain is *not* little!' she protested.

'Hmmm. It's hard to tell under all those curls...'

She propped herself up on one elbow and used her other hand to gather her corkscrewing hoard of curls into a tail at the nape of her neck. 'See! I've got a perfectly normal-sized head, containing a larger-than-average-sized brain!'

'Ha! That's not very logical, Lizzy...'

She snorted. 'The weight of the curls over the years has compressed the grey cells. It's actually more concentrated than most. You see?'

'You mean...' he murmured, as if overcome by wonder '...you mean there might be intelligent life in there?'

She pulled a face. 'A big head,' she continued, warming to her theme, 'is a sign of an inflated ego. *Not* of high intelligence. In my case, the balance is perfect. In your case, though, hats must be a real problem!'

'And what do *I* have to be big-headed about?'

'Oh-ho, Nicholas *Hartwood*! All that critical acclaim? Nominated for the Helmut Schreiber award last year? And what was it I read on the dust jacket of the first book? "An exciting new talent... The brightest and best of a rising generation of writers..."? Ha! *Now* try telling me you've got a hat that fits you!' Then she added, laughing, 'Woolly bobble-hats don't count.'

He stretched, then rolled over, presenting her with a view of his broad back.

She thought he was still playing the game. Pretending to be annoyed. So it came as a real shock when he spoke.

'And just when did you discover my *alter ego*?' His voice was gratingly low and hard.

'I...' She stopped herself. She felt like bursting into tears at the abrupt change of mood. She should never have asked that first question—never have tried to tease him into pretending to like her. It had been bound to end like this.

'I...' Oh, lord. She could hardly tell him she'd been snooping in his study. 'I don't know. I'd read your books ages ago. I'm a real fan. I guess it just sort of dawned on me...'

'Did it?' He had turned over on his back now. He was looking up at the sky. There was that shuttered look again.

She gazed across at him despairingly. 'Yes. Look, I'm sorry. I didn't know it was supposed to be some sort of secret. I wouldn't have mentioned it if I had. But I can't see why it matters. I'm desperately impressed, after all. I thought the books were wonderful. Honestly! I bought the second one in hardback, even though I couldn't really afford it, because the library said there was a long queue, and I couldn't bear to wait for the paperback to come out. That's why I remembered about you being nominated for that award. I was thrilled for you, long before I'd even met you! I think you're a brilliant writer, Nick. The jacket blurb didn't do you justice! You can't imagine how excited I was when I realised who you really were...'

He had sat up and was reaching out for his shirt. He didn't look cross or anything, now. He just looked like he always used to look when she was around. Before yesterday, that was. Not very interested. With something cynical and dry in the depths of his eyes.

Ah, well. She swallowed hard. The moment was over. This was where the difficult bit began. She had known, after all, that it was inevitable. Now she had to learn to keep out of his way. Except at night. And to keep her stupid, impetuous tongue under control. She had to learn to hide her love from him, and to stop wanting the impossible. If there had been anything to hand she would have thrown it at him.

Once they were dressed again Lizzy felt blindingly depressed.

From the moment he had closed her mouth with his kiss the previous evening they had been marooned in a magic world, cut off from all the worries and strife of the rest of their lives. Now they had stepped out of that charmed circle. Any minute now Nick would gather up the bags and they would walk down the mountainside to a harder reality.

She was groaningly hungry, and still too cold for comfort. Their house would be occupied by her awful parents for some time yet. And later, when they had gone away and they could raid the fridge and light the logs in the living-room grate, there would still be all the other problems to resolve. Only worse. Because now they were lovers. Would he still want her? And if he did, could she ever refuse him? And if she refused him, what then? The last time she had done that had been right here at the pool.

Nick had been cold and withdrawn afterwards, and the whole business had sent him haring off to a solicitor to try to get rid of her completely. Certainly he had warmed up a bit later, when he'd persuaded her to dodge the legal complications by marrying him. But it wasn't until the deed had actually been done and they were driving back to Mon Abri that she had seen, once again, the relaxed, lazy good humour that she felt was the real him. Or had been, that very first day, until she'd announced she was moving in. And that mood had only lasted until... until her parents had arrived. Her stomach lurched queasily as she realised just why he had been so furious with her the previous evening.

She had been too dismayed by her family's untimely arrival; too astonished by the spectacle of Nick discomfiting them; too overwhelmed by the discovery that she had fallen headlong in love with him to pay much attention to anything else that was said or done at the time. But now it all fell into place, and at last she understood.

She had reacted a little sourly to her parent's gloating announcement, simply recognising the delight they were taking in hurting her. But Nick must have known all along that one day they would find out that the house could be theirs. By marrying Lizzy he had thought he had killed two birds with one stone. He was safe from her claim, and ought to have been safe from theirs, too. After all, no normal, loving parents would ever sue their own daughter and her husband for their marital home! Now she knew why he had taken such pains to convince them that the marriage was a real love match... why he had brought her up the mountain for the night! He hadn't been the least bit generous towards her. And he hadn't tried to protect her, either. It was himself he had been looking out for all along.

No wonder he had been so angry when she tried to renounce her stake in the house. Only if she married him could he safeguard himself against a possible claim by her parents. And *they* weren't struggling to earn a living, with little more than a sour-faced van to their names. Her parents were well-to-do, to put it mildly. They, too, had the sort of clout that would make them formidable adversaries in a court of law. He had seen enough of them to realise that though they might have been intimidated by the implacable authority of his presence, it would be a different story once they were back in their own home, gossiping maliciously over a glass of port!

Once he had realised what they were really like he must have had a dreadful shock. That was when he had accused her so bitterly of protecting them . . . And that was why he had been so mad that she hadn't told him more.

Suddenly his marriage of convenience, designed to solve all the legal problems and secure him his house, had all rebounded on him. No longer did it protect him from the possibility of a long legal battle with an uncertain outcome. On the contrary, should her parents lose their case, he would now have to share the house with Lizzy. Not that she would take a penny, of course— but he wasn't to know that! Marrying Lizzy had been an empty gesture. How he must be kicking himself! The whole reason for the marriage was as null and void as her short-lived belief in her inheritance. No wonder he'd been so keen to make the most of having a wife in the physical sense! It was all he was going to get for his pains, after all.

Sitting on the grass, watching the waterfall, she had been getting gradually warmer. Suddenly she felt a sickening chill enter her bones. Yet another of her dreams was turning into a nightmare.

'Let's go,' said Nick, gathering the blankets together and slinging the holdall over his shoulder. He took a few steps towards the path, scarcely waiting for her to scramble to her feet. The long walk had begun.

He went upstairs to his study when they got back. Her parents had left. There was no sign that they had ever been there. Only the scars on Lizzy's soul. She wandered out to the workshop and sat at her wheel.

It was the first time she had turned her hand to anything except the planters for months. She worked the clay in her hands as she kicked the pedal on the wheel, setting it spinning far too fast. Then she locked her concentration fiercely on to the job in hand. She had the clay pliable. Now she had to get it properly centred.

He came to find her at lunchtime.

'That clay's grey,' he commented.

'Yes,' she said with a bright smile. 'It's still clay, though. I use it for my bowls...'

He nodded vaguely, then wandered off to the terrace to eat lunch. She dithered for a moment, wondering whether to join him or not. He was acting towards her pretty much as he'd always done. She'd better go. Otherwise he might begin to suspect . . .

Halfway through the meal something struck her. 'It was before ten when we arrived back here. And yet my parents had already gone. It's not like them . . .'

He looked steadily at her, his eyes cold. 'I arranged for a lawyer to call yesterday evening. To explain certain legal matters to them. Including the finer points of the laws of trespass in France. I also arranged for a firm to come and remove the tractor at dawn this morning. Their options were restricted.'

'Oh.' She put a hand to her face to hide a secret smile. It wasn't the notion of his discomfiting her parents that pleased her so much, but the realisation that he could have chosen to come back here as soon as they awoke. Instead, he had chosen to make love to her. Had she really imagined that she be able to resist continuing their affair? She began to look forward to dinner.

But he didn't eat dinner on the terrace with her that evening. He took his meal up to his study, instead. He said he had work to do. And then, alone, he went straight to bed.

Lizzy was glad she'd got her wheel out again. The orders still had to be filled, but every day she found a little time for her own work. It was a consolation, of sorts.

In her mind's eye she held an image of a very large, shallow bowl. She could see the exact curve—the exact proportions behind her closed lids. Day in, day out she let her hands try to recreate the line. She produced many

lovely bowls—but never the perfection for which she
strived. As each dish began to take shape on the wheel
she would discard the image, and let this particular piece
of clay follow its own destiny. She knew that she was
only a creator up to a point. Beyond that stage, the ma-
terial itself took over, and then she was merely a guide.

Nick came to watch, as he had always done. He was
always silent as he stood, observing her drawing the pale
grey clay up and out from the centre with her clever,
sensitive hands, or mixing the colours and glazes and
applying them with practised grace.

But that was all she saw of him. His deadline was fast
approaching, and he, too, was immersed in his work.
She didn't eat with him any more. Instead she cooked
her own meals and took them to the workshop or her
room. Wasn't that what they'd agreed on in the first
place? To live parallel lives without the one distracting
the other? She didn't want to speak to him, anyway. And
she certainly didn't want to look at him.

Though of course, occasionally, wrapped up in her
work, she would forget everything that had happened
and look up and catch him watching her steadily, leaning
against the door-jamb, his sleeves rolled back, his grey
eyes intent, and she would feel that old, familiar ache.
And then she'd drop her eyes to the clay, and kick the
pedal hard, and let her hands get back to work.

She even managed not to mind too much when he
went away again for a few days. He hadn't said where
he was going, this time. But she assumed he must be
returning to Montpellier and the stunning female *notaire*.

She didn't count the hours this time. Nor wake in the night. There was no point. There was nothing left to hope for.

The post had arrived. It brought three orders. Lizzy opened them on the terrace, puzzled.

'Something the matter?' asked Nick wryly.

'I've only got three orders today. And none at all yesterday. I assumed there'd been some sort of delay with the post and I'd get a double dose today. Is there some sort of strike going on? I haven't seen a newspaper for weeks.'

'No.' He took a sip of coffee, then set his mug down and leaned back in his seat.

'Are you sure?'

'What? About the strikes? No. How could I be? Anything could have happened in the last twenty-four hours.'

'Then why,' she muttered, irritated, 'did you say "no" so confidently?'

'Because world events are not the root cause of your diminished orders.'

She scoured his face in order to try to make some sense of his words. But he was giving nothing away.

'So...?' she said at last.

'So your ad didn't appear in the *Recorder* last week.'

'What?'

'No.'

'But why? What happened?'

He shrugged. 'When you first came you were appalled at the idea of moving half a mile down the road and yet not telling the *Recorder* of your change of address. So I took the precaution of telling them about your change of name and marital status. I knew you wouldn't have it any other way, Lizzy...'

She thought she might choke. 'How dare you?' she stuttered.

He smiled. 'You're always asking me that. He who dares wins, so they say——'

'Oh, shut up!'

'Certainly.'

There was a long silence while she chewed angrily at the corner of her mouth. But he was quite unperturbed, and clearly not about to elaborate further. In the end she sighed bitterly and asked, 'So why did you do it? Don't you believe in wives working, or something? Or did you just think it might be fun to strangle my business at birth?'

He tilted his head to one side as if he were considering his answer carefully, then he said, 'When men don't want their wives to work it's usually because they prefer them to spend their time massaging their male egos. So how about it, Lizzy?'

Anger sped through her, bringing her to her feet. 'For goodness' sake! I'm damned if I'd waste a minute of my time pandering to your inflated ego! Just tell me why you did it! For crying out loud! How could you do such a cruel thing? My business... My work...'

His features still impassive, he gestured her to sit down. But she folded her arms and continued to stand her ground.

'You speak,' he said evenly, 'as if your business and your work were one and the same thing. But the way I understand it, your business consists of you working sixteen hours a day as a one-woman production line, making your planters. It wears you out. In return it gives you money. Your work, on the other hand, absorbs you. It is leisurely. It can't be rushed. And the end product is quite beautiful. On the other hand it makes you no money.'

She frowned. 'So you don't approve of my making money?'

'Do you?'

She looked out towards the still line of the mountains. 'That's not the point,' she snapped.

He sighed. 'If you want to keep on with the planters... if you want to go on making money, then you'll find a list of shops in the kitchen on the dresser. Craft shops, in some of France's most expensive resorts. All of them have agreed to take your planters. In whatever quantity you can manage. No pressure. There's also the address of an art gallery which is desperately keen to display your bowls. But only if you agree to increase the price very substantially. Their clients, apparently, don't like to get something for nothing. It shakes their confidence in the investment potential of their purchases.'

She sat down, her legs shaking. Her heart was weeping. He *must* care a bit for her to have gone to all that trouble? 'Why did you do all that?' she whispered, trying to control the aching hope which trembled inside.

He lifted his eyes to meet hers. She could read nothing in their grey depths. 'Money... Prestige...' He paused, his mouth curling into a cold sneer. 'Well, Lizzy... You can have them in whatever proportions you decide to mix for yourself. And I shall be freed from the possible disruption of having you collapse on me. Now perhaps we can get down to discussing something a little more pressing.'

She conducted a little funeral inside her head for that stupid, shrivelled bud of hope. 'What do you mean, more pressing?' she asked weakly.

'The divorce.'

CHAPTER NINE

'YOU...you went to Montpellier to start the proceedings?'

'I went to see my lawyer to sort out a few things. And I started the ball rolling. Yes.'

'How long will it take?'

Nick shrugged. 'A while. Such things are always slow.'

'I see.' Lizzy puffed out her cheeks to prevent her mouth from doing something else. Like quivering. 'I...I don't have to stay here for the rest of the six months, now that my contract's void...' she added, a little more bleakly than she'd intended. She had meant to sound confident. Decisive.

'No,' he said sourly. 'You don't.'

So *that* was why he'd done it! Her dismay vapourised in the heat of her wrath. Right! She'd show him!

'However,' she continued coldly, 'we're married now. I don't know how one goes about getting a wife evicted from the marital home. But I don't imagine it can be easy.' She opened her eyes and wide and looked hard at him. 'Such things are always slow...' she added sarcastically.

Damn him. He didn't reply. She felt an overwhelming urge to goad the man into just the sort of rage that was brewing inside herself. But what did you have to say to him, for goodness' sake, to get him to react?

'It's a shame,' she remarked caustically, 'that we spoiled our chances of getting an annulment by—er—consummating our liaison. It might have been quicker.'

He tilted his head, thoughtfully. 'I doubt it...' he said, his mouth puckering into the beginnings of a cynical smile.

She sighed. If words wouldn't do it, she decided, then she'd try gestures. She clenched her teeth and sat tight. That was the answer! She was not going to budge from her seat. Too many of these discussions finished up with her turning on her heel and storming off. Well. She could sit there till nightfall, if need be. She'd *make* him feel uncomfortable in the end.

She growled inwardly. Fancy him telling the *Recorder* of her change of name so that she wouldn't have any excuse for staying! Of all the dirty, rotten tricks! How could she be so stupid as to love a man who was as ruthless as that?

He raised his eyebrows questioningly, and was just about to speak—though he still didn't look even mildly irritated—when the phone rang inside the house.

He stretched languidly before getting to his feet. 'If you'll excuse me, Lizzy,' he smiled, 'I'll just go and answer that.'

And he went indoors. And, what was more, he didn't come back. She could have gone on sitting there till nightfall, and he wouldn't even have known.

Her bitterness, thankfully, was mellowing. She hated the idea of harbouring a resentment. And as time passed she came to see more and more that Nick was, in some senses, an innocent victim. All he had wanted was his solitude in which to write. He was a brilliant writer. A skill such as his was hard come by. She knew that. So she couldn't blame him for trying to win back his freedom. She was the one who had insisted on staying, come what may. It would be wrong to blame him for doing whatever he could to resolve matters to his advantage—even to the point of using her to satisfy his lust. And it was hardly surprising that he had become so angry when it hadn't worked out.

She should go. Pack up her wheel and her kiln and find somewhere else. But she had come full circle. She had nowhere in the world to run to. And, anyway, she loved Nick far too much to go far away. Just bumping into him once a year on market day would be better than nothing.

She asked in the village about premises nearby. But the shopkeeper shook his head and confirmed what Nick had already told her. 'There is nowhere...I do not know why this should be. Perhaps we are all squirrels here in the mountains? We hoard things against a bad winter. Anyway, all the houses, the garages, the farm buildings...pfff.' He shrugged expressively. 'All are full, down from the ceiling to the floor.'

He came to the workshop one hot afternoon in late July. Sweat was running down Lizzy's brow from under the brim of her squashed and disreputable sun-hat. She hadn't noticed. This time the clay was behaving beautifully. This time the line was so close to the curve she carried in her mind's eye... If she just pulled it a tiny bit more like this...

'Lizzy?'

'Shut up! Shut up! Shut up!' she growled threateningly between clenched teeth, not daring to raise her eyes from her work. Just a little higher... The clay was perfect today... Just a little more... Just so... Like this...

He waited, in silence, until she had stopped the wheel spinning and was surveying the bowl.

'I didn't mean to break your concentration,' he said. Then he nodded at the bowl. 'That shape. It's amazing. Quite perfect.'

She kept her eyes on her work. He seemed to understand why she had been so rude. 'Nearly...' she sighed. 'Only nearly.'

He had come to bring out some letters for her. They were all to do with her work. Even Anna hadn't written for ages. But then, she thought ruefully, she hadn't written to Anna either. She was too used to telling Anna the truth about her life to begin dissembling now.

It wasn't until he had gone that she remembered what he had said about breaking her concentration. So he understood? Well, of course he did. He was a writer after all. All creative activities had that much in common at least. She'd never once disturbed him at his work for just that reason. And now she came to think of it he rarely spoke when he came to watch her at work... So even if he didn't rate her as a person, at least he acknowledged her properly as an artist...

But she trampled firmly on the very idea. It was just pointless and destructive, allowing herself to imagine that he would do anything solely for her own sake. He didn't speak to her because he had nothing to say to her. She was no more than an infuriating intrusion in his life. And a fool to allow her hopes to soar like that.

Instead she turned back to the bowl. What was it he'd said? Perfect... But it wasn't. It was only nearly perfect. And then her mind leapt back to that day at the pool, when he'd taken her on that picnic. What was it he'd said then? 'In the end, perhaps, you look back and decide that in all that struggle lay the very perfection that you thought was so elusive...' Something like that, anyway. So would she look back one day on this grey and tortured time and find perfection hiding there? Hardly! She laughed wryly. Well, at least it was nice to know he could be wrong sometimes.

A few days later he came by just as she was removing the bowl from the kiln.

'That's the one you were making the other day, isn't it?' he asked.

'How did you know?' she asked. It looked quite different now, fired to a high gloss, the proud bursts of colour jewel-bright.

He shrugged. 'Something about the shape, I suppose. I don't know.' Then he peered inside it. 'It's even better now it's finished. The colours are stunning.'

'Would you like it?' she said impulsively. 'Go on...' She thrust it towards him. 'Please. As a gift.'

But he looked at the bowl and then he looked at her and slowly shook his head.

The only reason that she didn't smash it hard upon the floor was her reluctance to let him know how she felt. Hurt that went that deep was a very private matter.

Should she go or should she stay? She sat in front of her wheel one stiflingly hot afternoon, mulling it over. Thunderclouds were gathering in the sky outside. There would be quite a storm. She could sense it in the air. In fact, she felt quite ill. She was surprised. Friends had often claimed that thundery weather made them feel odd, but she'd never experienced it. Yet today she felt quite sick, and very light-headed. She suddenly jammed her head down between her knees. There was a high-pitched singing in her ears, which took quite a time to die away. When she lifted her head again she felt awful. She stood up and shakily made her way to her room.

A cool shower and a glass of water settled her down. But the shower revealed something new and quite unusual. Her round, white breasts were lined with blue veins, and much fuller than they had ever been. Now she came to think of it, she'd been experiencing a strange, tingling sensation in her breasts recently, just as she'd been dropping off to sleep. She picked up her diary and thumbed through it...

The ringing in her ears began again. This time she actually fainted away on to the bed. Though whether it was the shock of the realisation, or her condition itself which was the cause of it, she really couldn't say...

The odd thing was, she was absolutely thrilled. She'd never dreamed of babies. She had been quite astonished when Anna had declared that it was all she wanted from life, now that she'd met John. As a schoolgirl, closeted away from the world, she had dreamed endlessly of the thrill of falling in love. But in all those dreams she had never once pictured herself with a tiny bundle in her arms.

Now that she let the image grow, she was tremblingly excited. For some reason, however bitter she had been about Nick's devious treatment of her, those hours she thought of as the 'magic journey' had never been tainted by her feelings. They stood apart in her mind, quite separate from all the rest. She had, for that brief night, been deeply and truly in love with Nick. And he had wanted her. She had seen it in his eyes. He had wanted

Lizzy Braithewaite that night, for reasons she would never know. Not because she was conveniently there and willing, but for her own self. What they had done, before the sun had set and after it had risen once more, had been absolutely and wonderfully right.

She already loved the baby that had been so magically conceived. But Nick must never know. She didn't want to be forced to have contact with him over the years concerning the child. It would be far, far too painful. And anyway—she picked up a copy of one of his novels which she kept beside her bed, and scanned a few pages— he needed his solitude. If he ever found out, then not just these few months, but the whole of the rest of his life would be beset by distractions.

It was several days before she finally plucked up the courage to go. She had left it too late in the day to head directly north. Instead she went first to Montpellier in the van and found a small, shabby hotel for the night. Tomorrow she would begin the long drive. She'd go back to London. It was wonderfully anonymous there. She had managed to smuggle quite a lot of her stuff into the van. She could get Anna to send for the rest of her things. Or pay some private haulage firm. She had a little money in the bank these days, after all, and could afford a gesture like that.

Anyway, somehow or another she could lay a false trail so that he'd never be able to find her. Not that he would bother to look. But she'd better make sure, for the baby's sake.

But when she tried to set off for Calais the following day the van refused to start. And it took a while to find a garage which was prepared to repair it. Even then the mechanic muttered disdainfully that it would take a long time to get parts. The model, he explained, had never been popular. Very few had been made. For some reason, people just didn't like driving these vans...

So she booked herself back into the hotel until the van was ready. And it was there, four days later, that Nick found her. She was lying on the bed, late in the afternoon, feeling drained and miserable. He didn't even knock—just flung open the door and stood looking at her.

He needed a shave. And his tan seemed to have faded. And his short, cropped curls were rumpled and spiky. She must have been miles away when he burst in, because she found herself thrilling instinctively to the sight of him. Until she reminded herself...

'What the hell are you doing here?' His voice was harsh, demanding.

She sat up. 'What does it look like? I'm sitting on the bed.'

'Oh, for God's sake!' and he came towards her and grasped her by the shoulders and shook her so that her hair fell forward across her face.

She pushed it back and looked at him defiantly, her green eyes huge.

'The time has come to stop this stupid posturing, Lizzy! You can snap out of that dreadful sulk right now!'

'I'm not sulking!' she returned, bewildered. What on earth was he doing here? And how in heaven's name had he found her?

But he wasn't listening. He had turned his back on her and was yanking her suitcase down from the top of the wardrobe. Then he flung open the wardrobe door and began to pile her clothes, complete with the hotel's hangers, into the case.

'Stop it!' she complained weakly.

He did stop. And he looked hard at the dishevelled heap of clothes.

'Who the hell do these belong to?' he asked in furious surprise.

'Me, of course! Who do you think they belong to?'

He looked across at her, raising one hand to smooth his rumpled hair. Then his shoulders dropped and the anger seemed to evaporate from his eyes. He raised his brows. 'Well, not Charlton Hesketh, that's for sure...' he drawled.

She wanted to laugh. But she didn't dare. It might annoy him again. She had found his turbulent entrance extremely disturbing. She preferred to cultivate this more benign mood.

'They *are* my clothes. What's so mysterious about them?'

He pushed the wardrobe door closed with his shoulder, and leaned against it, arms folded. It was faced with a full-length mirror, so that she could see his back as well as his front while he stood surveying her in that old, familiar posture. It was just as well she hadn't known his back looked that good, propped against the door-jamb. She might have fallen in love with him twice as quickly, and had twice as long to suffer...

'I've never seen you wear them. That's what's so odd,' he said drily, looking down again at the pile of nineteen-thirties dresses in the suitcase.

'I used to wear them quite a lot before I arrived at Mon Abri. But I thought I'd be less of a distraction in shorts and T-shirt!'

'Less of a distraction! Lizzy! These dresses are un-believably demure compared to your shorts! Those legs of yours have been driving me crazy! I thought I'd mentioned that little fact?'

'Er—yes... You did. But you didn't mean it. My legs are so pale...' She wasn't going to start getting her hopes up. Just because he'd turned up and said he liked her in shorts didn't mean anything had really changed.

'Of course they're pale. You're a redhead. What colour did you think I'd expect them to be?'

He lifted his hands to his face and rubbed them raspingly over his unshaved jaw. Then he went over to the chest of drawers and began tumbling her underwear into the case. She winced with embarrassment.

'What are you doing here, anyway?' she asked tentatively, hoping to distract him from the sight of that aquamarine silk, all wrapped up in pink tissue paper...

He looked up, a wry expression on his face. 'I've brought you your mail. Why did you think I'd come?'

She thought she'd risk a laugh this time, but he straightened up abruptly and pulled a letter from the back pocket of his jeans. It hadn't been a joke. The envelope was grubby and dog-eared, but even from a distance she could see her name engraved on it in a handsome copperplate. She'd only ever known one person who wrote like that. And he'd been dead for over a year. She stared at it with eyes suddenly brimful of tears.

He slipped it back into his pocket. 'Read it on the way home,' he said gently.

She blinked hard, but the action tipped a solitary tear on to her short, freckled nose. He came across and lifted it away with the tip of one finger. Then he put the finger to his lips.

'Come on, Lizzy. Help me pack.'

Obediently she scrambled off the bed and knelt beside the suitcase.

They didn't speak again until the Range Rover was gathering speed on the road towards the mountains.

'How did you find me?'

'Cyclops. Or indirectly, at least.'

'The van?'

'Yes. I couldn't figure out how you'd managed to flood the engine that first day. I suspected the thermostat. Anyway, I figured the van would never see you all the way back to England. So I contacted the manufacturers, and traced a request for parts to a small garage in Montpellier. The rest was easy.'

'Oh.' That bloody van. She knew she'd been right not to trust it.

She'd been unbelievably wishy-washy, letting him lead her away like a docile lamb, and all because he had an old letter for her from Grandpa in his pocket. She should have demanded the letter in a peremptory fashion and sent him packing. After all, with the baby coming she'd have to run away again soon. It couldn't be long before it would start to show—though she had no real idea about how long these things took. But, in any case, he must never, ever find out.

'There must have been easier ways of getting the letter to me?'

'Quite probably.'

'So why did you take the hard route? That's surely not your style.'

'Because I had to bring you both back home, of course.'

The blood froze in her veins. 'Both...?' she whispered cagily.

'Yes. You are pregnant, aren't you?'

Her lips had stuck together. She had to moisten them with the tip of her tongue before she spoke. 'How did you...I mean...I... What on earth makes you think *that*?'

'If you're going to go on being pregnant for the next nine months—or eight?—or whatever?—you'd better learn to be sick more quietly in the mornings. You make a terrible din.'

Damn. She'd only been sick twice. It was partly that which had made her decide to go in such a hurry in the end. But she thought she'd been pretty quiet about it, all things considered. Bionic hearing, obviously, too.

'Even so, I don't know what makes you think——'

'That it's any of my business? Well, unless it's a phantom pregnancy, engendered by your phantom lover, Charlton, then I consider it's very much my business. Don't you?'

'Not really, no. I don't.'

'Well, I do. And in case you've got any plans about bringing it up alone, then let me warn you that if you stick to your guns you'll have to bring it up in the outhouse. Because you're neither of you leaving Mon Abri.'

'Then you can move the pig-nuts as soon as we get back,' she muttered crossly. 'And get that lawyer of yours to come and see me one evening and explain the finer points of the laws of kidnap in France.'

He didn't reply. He just kept his eyes fixed grimly on the road ahead. But even in profile she could see that he was very angry indeed.

*   *   *

By the time he led her into the sitting-room and forced her to sink back into the plump cushions of the sofa, she had quite got over the excitement of his coming all that way to find her, and saying what he had about her legs. It was the baby who had finally roused him into positive action. Not her. He'd probably even faked Grandpa's letter to use as a carrot to get her into the car. One lot of copperplate, after all, looked pretty much like another.

She didn't ask to see the letter. The disappointment of finding out the truth would be more than she could bear. She'd soon get used to the idea, though... She'd got used to a lot worse than that in the past weeks alone.

He brought her a coffee, and sat facing her on the sofa opposite, leaning forwards slightly, his forearms folded across his knees.

'Are you allowed to drink coffee?' he asked. His face broke into a foolish smile of delight as he said it, the lines carving deep into his cheeks.

She shrugged. 'I don't know. I think so.'

'We'll have to find out all these sorts of things...' he said with satisfaction, the smile broadening.

'Don't look so pleased! Please don't! I can't bear it!'

'But I am pleased. I can't help myself!'

'But you don't understand, Nick. I don't know the first thing about babies.'

'I shouldn't have thought you'd let a little thing like that worry you, Lizzy. After all you didn't know the first thing about running a business, either, and you didn't let that stop you?'

What was he saying now? 'Are you suggesting that I should have done something about contraception? Because if so, can I ask you to cast your mind back and——?'

'Well,' he interrupted cheerfully, leaning back in the chair and locking his fingers behind his neck in an attitude of supreme relaxation, 'I *did* think you might have been prepared. What with Charlton——'

'You knew there was no Charlton!'

'No, I didn't. Well, yes, I did, after a while. But when you told me about the mystery Romeo of Albi I thought Charlton might just have been a cover-story for the real thing. I didn't know for sure until we made love.'

'So you *are* blaming me!'

'No. For goodness' sake, Lizzy! What an appalling thing to say. I *wanted* to make love with you. And if you want the truth, then I not only never gave contraception a second thought, but I would have been hurt and disappointed if I'd thought you had. It wasn't like that, was it? Why? Are you blaming me?'

'No. Of course I'm not blaming you. And I'm delighted that there's a baby coming. But you still don't understand . . .'

'So I'm delighted. You're delighted. Where's the problem?'

'You *don't* understand, Nick. I don't know anything at all about handling babies. Let alone triplets.'

'Triplets!' He stood up so fast she felt the air move. He stared at her in wide-eyed astonishment. The smile had quite disappeared from his face. 'You mean,' he croaked huskily, 'you're having triplets?'

Oh, dear. At long last she'd managed to wring a spontaneous response from him by something she'd said. But she hadn't meant *that* at all. It was just the way it had come out.

'Not exactly. No. Well, I mean, I might be——'

'For God's sake, Lizzy! What did the doctor say?'

'Nothing. I mean, I haven't seen a doctor yet.'

'Then how the hell——?'

'Listen! Nick, please listen.' He slumped back into the sofa, his eyes fixed on her face.

'I didn't really mean you to think I was having triplets. It was just the way it came out. But the point is, I *might* have triplets. Or quads. Anybody could. Though they're quite rare, so it isn't exactly likely. But what I'm trying to say is... think how they'll distract you from your work... Even a single baby can be a terrible distraction. Especially when the mother doesn't know what she's doing... But triplets would be a disaster...'

'Now it's your turn to listen, Lizzy. I already love this baby... Whether it's a her or a him or a them. And I want the baby to distract me! Or all three of them, if that's how it turns out.'

'Yeah...' she sighed despondently. He was missing the point completely. She might not know much about babies, but it seemed she knew more than he did. 'You want it to giggle and gurgle and make you laugh. Sure. Everybody loves to be distracted like that. But have you ever heard a baby with colic?'

'Colic? I thought that was what horses got?'

'And babies. Well, some babies anyway. It makes them cry non-stop for three months, apparently.'

He shrugged. 'I've put up with you crashing about this place for quite a while and my hair's not grey. Yet. I love my baby, Lizzy. If she gets colic I shall feel sorry for her, and hold her tight to let her know I care, and try not to let the noise tug at my heart-strings too much.'

Lizzy turned her head sharply to one side, so that he wouldn't see the way her nostrils were quivering. She swallowed two or three times. She couldn't even begin to imagine her own parents saying something like that. She was going to give birth to the luckiest baby in the world. It had hardly started growing yet and already both its parents loved it enough to put up with the colic!

She stood up, abruptly, and headed for the stairs.

'Lizzy?' His voice was gentle, cajoling. 'Where are you going?'

'I think,' she sighed, without turning her head, 'I think I feel a bit sick.'

He was there, in an instant, at her shoulder, one arm coming around her to support and cradle her. 'Do you really feel sick?' he asked softly.

'No,' she said. And then she began to cry.

CHAPTER TEN

NICK refused to discuss anything any more. He said she was tired and needed her rest, insisted on making her a light meal and brought it up to her room on a tray.

When he had taken her by the elbow to her room, Lizzy's heart had sunk heavily with disappointment. She hadn't allowed herself to recognise the knot of excitement which had been tangling itself ever tighter in her stomach since he'd burst into that hotel-room looking...well, not like his usual self, anyway.

She surely hadn't expected him to take her to his bed, had she? After all, she'd only been brought back here as a vessel for the child she was carrying. He wanted the baby. And he couldn't have one without the other. The only thing he liked about her was her legs. And her womb.

She ate a little of the meal, and then pushed the rest away. She cried a little bit more into her pillow. But it kept reminding her of the glorious luxury of sobbing against his broad chest.

What was it he'd said? 'You can cry on my shoulder if you want to, Lizzy. It's OK.' But she hadn't been able to, after all. He was too tall. She'd had to make do with his chest, and a fine mess she'd made of his shirt while she was about it. Tomorrow, she vowed, as she drifted on the edge of sleep, she'd get her life sorted out. And she'd do it properly this time.

She slept late. Very late. But at least she appeared to have slept through the hour when she'd been experiencing the morning sickness. She felt hungry when she woke. By the time she trailed wearily out on to the terrace she was ravenous.

He appeared before she'd even had a chance to sit down.

'How're you feeling?' he asked.

'OK,' she replied with a weak smile. 'Hungry.'

'I'll bring breakfast out...'

He was remarkably swift. Swift enough for her to start imagining that he must have begun making the coffee when he'd heard the first creak of the floorboards upstairs. But if he had done, she reflected, then it was simply so that the baby wouldn't have to wait for its breakfast. Not for her.

The tray was laid out with coffee and croissants and butter and apricot jam. Just like that first morning. But in the centre of the tray, this time, was a very large bowl of fruit. A nearly perfect bowl.

She pointed at it. 'How did you get it? I sent it off to the shop in Marseilles. Did you tell them I'd changed my mind or something?'

He shook his head. 'I bought it. Though I had a bloody difficult time tracing it. Why didn't you send it to the gallery, after I made all those arrangements?'

She looked at him in disbelief. 'But...' He'd turned it down when she'd offered to give it to him! The pain of that moment jabbed into her afresh.

'The gallery wanted to charge far too much for them,' she muttered fiercely. 'Even so, it still cost an awful lot of money! You can't just put fruit in it and plonk it on the table!'

'It's mine, now. I can do what I like with it, surely?'

Oh, damn him. Damn and blast him to the other side of the universe! It was *her* bowl. Her nearly perfect bowl. The only one she'd ever made. She'd offered to give it to him, for goodness' sake, and he'd turned it down. And now he'd twisted things round by buying it, so that it was *his* bowl. His. But free from the taint of having been given, as a gift, by her. Though she was glad, in her heart, that he was using it, and hadn't locked it away in a glass-fronted cabinet.

She had always tried to price her goods as cheaply as possible, partly so that people would feel OK about using them. The gallery's prices would have made them too outrageously expensive for her to even consider using them as an outlet. But even the shops which took her planters had insisted on a far higher price for the bowls than she would have liked. And now, on top of everything, he'd gone and made her say the opposite of what she really believed. He'd had made a liar of her yet again!

She sloshed some coffee into her cup and slurped it noisily. It was no good. He might have her nearly perfect bowl. But he wasn't going to have *her*.

'I think we'd better discuss the future,' she said archly, rubbing the tip of her scalded tongue over her lips to cool it down.

'Yes?' He was sitting opposite her now, sipping cautiously at his own cup.

'I'm not going to stay here, you know. You can't make me.'

He looked at her thoughtfully, his face half-serious, half-sad. Then he produced the dog-eared envelope from a pocket and laid it on the table in front of her.

'I think you'd better read this, Lizzy.'

She picked it up and fingered it. She'd been wrong. One copperplate hand was not a bit like any other. She'd know her grandfather's writing anywhere. All those years at boarding-school. All those letters.

'Where did you get it?' she whispered.

'Jean-Claude. Your grandfather left a letter for each of us with him. He was supposed to deliver them to us on our wedding day. Or when we'd been living here together for six months. Whichever came sooner. But we kept our wedding fairly quiet, if you remember. And Jean-Claude had been closing his ears to gossip about us, because he was embarrassed about the money you'd sent him... Anyway, eventually he listened to the local scandal-mongers and his conscience got the better of him.'

'Oh.' She stared at the letter, her mind a blank. 'But how could Grandpa have known I'd turn up here?'

'You'd better read it, Lizzy, and find out.'

He wrote as he spoke. He always had. She could hear his gravelly voice ringing in her ears as she struggled to make sense of the words on the page.

My darling, dearest Lizzy,

So you're reading this, which can only mean that my little plot has worked! Ha! See what a fine man I found for you, Lizzy! I had to go halfway round the world before I met a man good enough for you. Not that I was on the look-out, you understand, but when he popped up in that bar and we got talking I just couldn't help but think of you and him together.

Grandma nearly bit my head off when I told her, of course, but she's come round in the end. She said you'd hate the idea of my meddling like that. But I pointed out that all I was doing was making the pair of you sit up and take notice of each other. Nothing more than that. The rest was in the lap of the gods. But if you've got to the stage of reading this then I must have been right. And I couldn't see how to get the two of you together any other way.

He was the best man I ever met in all my long life, Lizzy. And yet, there he was, determined to turn Mon Abri into a monastery, just to produce a few more books to add to the libraries of the world. I told him, that house is not meant for single occupation! I even spun him some yarn about me planting out the garden for Grandma, though anybody who knew how I felt about gardening wouldn't have been fooled for a minute. Grandma would have smacked me over the head if she could have heard me! I told him he'd never know a moment's true happiness without a wife to share it with. I told him all about Grandma and me and how happy we are.

But he was stuck on some idea about the dignity and strength of the victims of war he'd encountered on his assignments. He said everyone he'd met since was just like milk and water in comparison. He was going to live for his work—to prove that hope *did* exist for those poor souls. That was all.

I started arguing, but I could see he meant what he said. And then I thought of you, Lizzy. All spunk and fire and gritty determination. And when I came to think a bit deeper I realised that you were the product of warfare, too, in a very different sort of way, of course. So maybe he *had* hit on some kind of truth, after all. He has a way, as you'll have discovered, of being right.

Anyway. There you were—the dearest girl in all the world, turning up your nose at all the men who came chasing after you. And there he was, just the kind of man who could handle a firecracker like you without getting his fingers burned.

Lizzy paused, her eyes filled with foolish tears. She couldn't look at Nick, although she was conscious that he was watching her—almost living each word with her. The letter continued:

So what should I have done about it? Be honest, Lizzy, if I'd invited the pair of you round for afternoon tea, you'd have both smiled politely and paid no real attention to each other whatsoever. I'm right, aren't I?

Anyway, I'd already half agreed to sell him the house before I even got the idea. I needed the money to pay my passage to Papua New Guinea, you see. Grandma had had the house made over to me so that I could use it to raise cash on my trips if I ever needed to, but we'd made a point of saying nothing in the family, because we had an idea your mother and father would have made a fuss.

So we made out this contract and I just stuck in a little bit about it being conditional on my wife's agreement, and then when I got back home I got the solicitors to make out a proper contract with this extra clause in it. The idea was that if within one year of your meeting each other you were neither wed nor living together then the house would have to be sold and the proceeds split between you.

But I got it all put in that strange legal language they use and then had it all translated into legal French which is a hundred times worse and then I had it typed up in the tiniest print you ever saw and then I sent out the contract for him to sign at a time when I'd found out he was up to his eyes in meeting some publisher's deadline. Pretty clever, don't you think? Grandma and me sweated a bit until we got the contract back all signed and sealed. The shame of it is that it's obvious we won't be around to see how it all works out in the end.

But don't grieve for us, my darling. We've had joy and happiness every inch of the way. And you were the best thing of all the good things that ever happened in our lives.

So don't go losing your temper with us, Lizzy. We loved you too dearly to just stand back from your life and let you go it alone. And it's been especially hard since we've known we won't be around for you much longer.

But now you've got the best man in the world to love and cherish you, so you can stop fighting and get on with living. Just the idea that it might all work out has cheered the pair of us up no end, you know?

So be happy, my dear one, and give that Nick a punch in the ribs from me. With all my dearest love, your own...Grandpa.

Lizzy folded the letter carefully and put it back in the envelope. She was too choked to speak. She kept her eyes fixed on her hands, as they smoothed the edge of the envelope, back and forth.

'Well?' Nick was leaning across, his eyes clear and steady.

She looked up at him. 'Well?' she echoed huskily.

'What do you think of the letter?'

'You know what's in it, if he left one for you, too?'

'Pretty much. I don't suppose they're very different in essentials.'

'No. I don't suppose they are.'

'So what do you think?'

She looked at him wide-eyed with despair. 'What am I supposed to think? I think that my grandparents were the best people in the world. And it helped them in their last months to think that they'd found a way to make me safe after they had gone... It's a shame it hasn't worked out.'

'Is that all, Lizzy? Is that all you think?'

'Yes. Of course.' She shrugged. 'When you went to see the *notaire* the first time you would have discovered about that clause, I suppose. It doesn't really change anything, though. You still married me to make sure you wouldn't lose the house.'

He stood up and wandered to the edge of the terrace, looking out over the balustrade to the valley beyond. He had his back to her, his shoulders hunched.

His voice when it came was thick with anger. 'God damn it, Lizzy. Is that all you've got to say? I've been like a cat on bricks waiting to give you that letter. I thought it would force you to say...*something*! Instead you're keeping up that pathetic sulking to the bitter end! What does it take to get through to you?'

She bit her lip. 'I'm not sulking. Honestly.'

He swung around to face her, his face grim and his eyes flashing fire. 'Aren't you? Aren't you sulking, Lizzy Holt? Because that's what it seems like to me. Ever since we made love you've been withdrawn like this. I thought I understood. And I tried to be patient. After all, you'd wanted to save your virginity for a man you loved, and I'd robbed you of that! But what happened is past, Lizzy. And I can't bring myself to regret it, so you'll *never* wring that apology you want from me.'

She was shocked almost into silence. But not quite. 'I don't want you to apologise. And I don't regret it, either. And I haven't been sulking!'

'Then what the hell have you been doing?'

It was on the tip of her tongue to cry out that she'd been breaking her heart. But she managed to catch the words back in time.

He let the breath out of his body in a shuddering sigh. 'For crying out loud! You've had me tied in knots since you arrived here that very first day, looking like an angel and fighting like a demon!'

'I've had *you* tied in knots!' She made an explosive sound with her mouth.

'Yes. That boyfriend! I *believed* in him, Lizzy. I even believed in his stupid name! Though I have to admit, I didn't think he sounded much of a challenge. Except perhaps for his lineage! I thought if I just waited you'd soon realise... It was only when I tried to trace this old family name of his that I realised he didn't even bloody exist! That the one woman I'd...I'd really *wanted* in my life had turned me down in favour of a...a...goose-necked phantom!'

That was odd. She'd always imagined Charlton with a goose neck, too. She didn't comment on it though. Instead she asked sourly, 'So why did you care about his lineage?'

'I didn't care about his lineage. But I thought you might have done. You said something about your own name being commonplace when I first met you. That sort of stuff is important to some people.'

'So you thought I was the sort of person who cared about that sort of thing. Tremendous.'

'Lizzy—for crying out loud! You were the one who mentioned his lineage. And you sounded so proud when you said it!'

'Of course I sounded proud! I'd just thought it up! I was proud of myself for thinking up a proper lie! You can't imagine the hot water I've got into in my life because I was so hopeless at lying.' Then she added bitterly, 'Anyway, I said my mother thought our family name was important! Not me! Like mother, like daughter, huh?'

'But I didn't know what your mother was like, Lizzy! Not then! And when I did...' He tailed off. His face darkened with that frightening anger she had seen only once before. 'And when I did, Lizzy...it...it almost broke me up. I've never been so bloody angry in all my life!'

His hands knotted into hard fists, the knuckles white against the brown of his skin.

So she'd been right...her parents...he'd thought he could secure the house...

And then something seemed to burst inside her mind. She grappled with the contents of Grandpa's letter. She had been wrong. Her reasoning had been wrong. Nick had known about the clause in her grandfather's contract when he'd asked her to marry him. He knew perfectly well that her parents had no right to the house at all. So why had he been so furious? Not just because they were so rude. He wasn't the kind of man to let a pair of lightweights like that get under his skin.

'So why did it bother you so much to discover what my parents were like?'

He was storming now. Glaring at her, his features set and hard, his fists clenched. 'Because I couldn't bear it!' A fist crashed down upon the table, setting the nearly perfect bowl rocking. 'I couldn't bear the idea that you'd had to live twenty-four years on this earth with...with scum like that for your family! I couldn't bear the idea that there was something terrible like that in your life and you wouldn't share it with me. Lizzy! Can't you understand?'

'I...' Oh, dear. She was having to try very hard *not* to understand. Because she knew all about what happened when she let herself hope that Nick cared about her...

'I...wanted you that night, Lizzy...' His voice was thick, clotted with emotion. 'I wanted you so badly. I wanted to make love to you and make things right for you and...' He took in a sharp breath. 'For me it was a kind of symbolic wedding night...I believed we could go forward from there, because the big secret in your life was out and...there would be nothing left to keep you from seeing the truth...' He started to breathe harder, his eyes reaching into her own.

'But afterwards, Nick. You...you froze on me. When we were talking. I was so happy and then you...well...' she shrugged weakly, pleadingly.

'Yes. Well. I've always tried not to believe in fairy-stories. Perhaps it was all a bit too much like a happy ending. I was afraid of trusting in it too much. Certainly that was what I thought when you started making such a fuss about my writing. I thought I'd married a fierce little warrior. And I found I'd married a fan. Or at least, that was how it seemed.' There was a bitter cast to his expression when he said that.

She sighed. Then she ran her fingers through her hair pushing it back from her face. 'I thought you'd married an adversary in law, Nick. To save your home.'

He came to sit opposite her. His fingers slowly unknotted. His hands fell, curling easily, into his lap. He was silent.

'Why,' she asked nervously, 'should it have mattered what I thought of your work? When I was nothing more than a legal technicality?'

He was watching her, more guardedly now. 'Lizzy, when I went to see the lawyer I found out about your grandfather's hidden clause. But I wasn't frightened of losing the house when the year was up. I couldn't have cared less, by then, about the bloody house. I was frightened that when you found out that your grandmother's bequest was meaningless you'd toss that proud little head of yours and march off. And I'd never see you again. Your grandfather wasn't the only one to cook up a little plot to make you take notice.'

'Oh.' She wrinkled up her nose. 'So you didn't think I was after you for your money?'

He laughed. An explosive, disbelieving laugh. 'Lizzy Holt! Nobody who can choose to drive a van like yours can be over-concerned with the things that money can buy! A less improbable money-grubber I have yet to meet!'

'But you *did* think I'd married you for prestige!'

He looked ever so slightly shame-faced at that one. 'Yes. Well. The gallery soon put me right about that when I rang them up to secure your bowl. No one who had it in them to say what you'd said to one of the top art dealers in France could be over-concerned about prestige, either.'

He paused. Then he looked stoically at her and asked, 'So why did you marry me, Lizzy? And I want the truth, this time.'

'Why,' she asked, her face set and determined, 'did you buy my bowl?'

There was a long, long pause. And then he said, 'My question first. If you answer my question, I'll answer yours.'

She met his eyes boldly. He who dares, wins...she found herself thinking.

'Because I believed the house was immensely important to your work. And I believed your work was immensely important to you. And I cared that you should have what you wanted...needed...' She looked down. Her nerve had fled.

He stood up and came to stand behind her. Then he put his hands on her shoulders and his face in her hair. And he said softly, 'I bought your bowl because you had gone. If I hadn't got you back... Well, let's just say I wanted you a damn sight more than I wanted that bowl. And if the wretched pot wasn't so perfect I'd smash it on the floor to prove my point.'

'That bowl,' she whispered, 'like our child, is obviously destined to be. It's used up two lives already.'

He stood there for a long time. He breathed into her hair until the blood roared in her veins. Until the throb of desire threatened to choke her.

Then he said, 'I love you, Lizzy *Braithewaite*. I know it's probably an embarrassment to you, and you don't feel the same way at all. But I love you, and I can't keep the words hidden any longer.'

'The name's *Holt*,' she reminded him, letting her lip quiver in time to the music which was singing in her ears. 'I'm not a bit embarrassed, for reasons which I shall leave you to guess at. And I've got something for you from Grandpa.' And with that she dug her elbow in his ribs as hard as she dared.

He pulled her to her feet and came to face her, his hands still tight on her shoulders. 'And I've got something for you, from him, as well…' And with that his face came down to meet hers and his lower lip, when it touched hers, was shaking just a little bit, too.

Later, much later, when the sunlight through the louvred shutters was painting tiger's stripes on the milky surface of her skin, he asked, 'Do you really love me, Lizzy?'

'More than words can say,' she smiled happily.

'Even though I've got French arms?'

She ran a finger along the line of muscle from his wrist to his elbow. The sleek, dark hairs, one after another, stood up on end.

'Especially,' she breathed, 'because you've got French arms.'